The Type-A Guide to Natural Disasters

A Sunset Ridge Cozy Mystery, Volume 3

Elizabeth Spann Craig

Published by Elizabeth Craig, 2025.

This is a work of fiction. Similarities to real people, places, or events are entirely coincidental.

THE TYPE-A GUIDE TO NATURAL DISASTERS

First edition. July 8, 2025.

Copyright © 2025 Elizabeth Spann Craig.

ISBN: 978-1955395588

Written by Elizabeth Spann Craig.

Chapter One

Thunder cracked overhead as Arlo launched himself through the blue tunnel. His small body was a blur of determination despite legs that seemed too short for agility work. The sky had turned an unnatural yellowish-green in the last ten minutes, casting an eerie light over the training field.

"Go, Arlo, go!" Sam Prescott called, her voice nearly lost in the sudden gust that sent the course flags snapping violently. The wind whipped her dark hair across her face as she ran alongside the course, signaling the next obstacle.

Arlo, who was an improbable mix of basset hound and cavalier King Charles spaniel, navigated the weave poles with surprising grace, his soulful eyes locked on Sam's every movement despite the chaos around them.

"Look at him go!" Lucy shouted from the sidelines, her own whippet Ziggy pressing anxiously against her legs. "He's getting faster every week."

But as Arlo cleared the final jump, another thunderclap boomed directly overhead, drowning out the cheers from the remaining club members. Equipment rattled ominously across the field.

Dave jogged over, his border collie Rocket already herding the smaller dogs toward the parking area. "That's it, folks. The storm's moving in faster than predicted." He glanced at the menacing sky. "Where did this come from? It wasn't supposed to hit until tonight."

The dogs seemed to have picked up on the storm faster than the humans had. They'd pinned their ears back and turned their faces toward the sky before their owners had noticed anything other than gusty wind. Ziggy, the whippet, had tucked his tail between his legs and was pressing his slender body firmly against Lucy's legs.

Sam knelt to clip Arlo's leash. The little dog pressed against her leg, his usual post-run joy dampened by the electric feeling in the air.

"We need to get this equipment secured now," Ginny called, her wild red curls whipping around her face as she struggled with the tunnel that had begun to roll across the field.

As Sam sprinted to help, her phone buzzed with an emergency alert. The words "Severe Weather Warning" flashed across her screen.

They quickly packed up everything, struggling against the wind as they did.

As Sam finished packing up Arlo's gear at the agility field, Ginny approached with her Jack Russell terrier, Pixie.

"Arlo's getting faster every week," Ginny said as she bent to give the little dog a scratch behind the ears. "Hey, you should bring Franklin again next time. That kid has a natural way with dogs."

"I'll see if Lisa can spare him," Sam replied, smiling at the memory of Franklin's excitement the last time he'd attended. Franklin Smith was the young neighbor boy who occasionally helped walk Arlo when Sam was busy. They'd bonded after he'd shown up on her doorstep in tears after missing his school bus last year.

"Well, he's welcome anytime," Ginny said.

With the storm firing up quickly, the group headed on their separate ways, dogs in tow. The rain pounded relentlessly against the windshield.

Arlo looked anxiously at Sam from his perch in the backseat. She glanced at him in the rear-view mirror. "It's okay, little boy. We're heading home to ride it out."

The whole scenario was an odd one. A late-season hurricane from the gulf took a sharp turn and headed for the Appalachian Mountains. It was supposed to come the following day. It should have meant just a bit of heavy rain and maybe some straight-line winds as it allegedly turned into a tropical depression. But as Sam drove back home, her phone started shrieking at her with another emergency alert. Arlo gave a sharp bark in response, and Sam spoke to him soothingly.

The steep and winding driveway to her home seemed longer than usual. Cresting the hill, Sam's historic brick house came into view. The stately columns and arched windows now looked vulnerable against the rapidly blackening sky. The grand veranda that had charmed her when she'd purchased the property now seemed like a liability, its roof already collecting debris flung by the strengthening gusts.

Lightning illuminated the wrought-iron fence surrounding the property, casting spidery shadows across the lawn.

She pulled directly into the garage, not wanting to leave her car exposed. Arlo whined softly from the backseat, his usual composure replaced by an alertness that Sam had rarely seen since the days after she'd rescued him.

"Don't worry," Sam said, gathering her agility bag and unclipping Arlo's harness. "We're Type-A prepared for this, remember?"

Inside, the house already felt different, almost as if it were bracing itself. The tall windows in the sunroom rattled with each new gust, and the ornate chandelier in the foyer swayed almost imperceptibly. The century-and-a-half-old structure had weathered countless storms, but today felt like something different.

Arlo dashed to the kitchen and back, his nails clicking frantically on the hardwood floors. Outside, a lawn chair from somewhere down the hill tumbled across Sam's front yard, followed by what looked like someone's garbage can lid spinning like a frisbee.

Sam headed straight for her emergency supply closet. Hurricane or not, she had a laminated checklist and enough supplies to outlast whatever was coming. At least that's what she kept telling herself as another emergency alert buzzed through the silent house.

Her phone rang right after the alert stopped and as she was pulling out emergency lanterns from the closet. She wasn't surprised to see it was Olivia. Olivia had been through a lot recently and had made an amazing recovery from a violent encounter she'd barely survived. Her brother, Jason, had moved out just recently and was renting a place in town after acquiring a job at the credit union, leaving Olivia in her large home alone. Basically, the last thing Olivia needed was a major storm. She'd been through enough of them.

"You made it home?" Olivia asked without preamble. "Lucy called and said the agility club nearly blew away."

"Barely," Sam said, shifting the phone to her shoulder as she continued inventory. "Arlo and I practically swam to the car. How are you holding up?"

"I'm fine, but Jason's freaking out a little. He's never been through anything like this. He was trying to tape up the windows in his apartment."

"Tell him the tape doesn't actually help," Sam said. "Old wives' tale. But moving his car away from those massive oaks near his apartment building would be smart."

"He told me he'd done that," Olivia replied. "I've been trying to get ready for the storm, too. Before you ask, I've filled the bathtub with water."

"Look at you, turning into a proper prepper," Sam said, genuinely impressed.

Olivia laughed, the sound still precious to Sam after the attack that had left her fighting for her life just weeks earlier. "I learned from the best, didn't I? Though I can't find that hand-crank radio you gave me."

"Bottom of the hall closet, blue emergency bin," Sam replied automatically, then winced at herself.

But Olivia just chuckled. "I had the feeling you'd remember." A crash sounded in the background. Then, suddenly, the line went dead.

Sam stared at her phone. Was that the first power outage sign, or just bad connection?

A tremendous crack of thunder sent Arlo scurrying under the dining room table, his small body trembling violently.

"Hey, little guy," Sam said, dropping to her knees. "It's just noise," she said gently.

But those soulful eyes told her he wasn't totally convinced. Before Sam rescued him, Arlo had spent his life chained in a front yard, exposed to every element nature could throw at him. His previous owner had left him out through thunderstorms, blizzards, and blistering heat—all while the man stayed comfortably inside.

"Not on my watch," Sam whispered, sliding completely under the table to sit beside him. She stroked his soft ears, feeling his racing heart gradually slow under her touch.

The storm hit full force around nine that evening. Sam and Arlo huddled in the interior hallway as the wind screamed around the house's corners. Her generator kicked on automatically when the power failed, but the sturdy brick walls couldn't mask the sounds of the destruction outside—cracking trees, the metallic screech of something large being torn apart, car alarms wailing briefly before going silent.

Midnight brought the eye of the storm and tempted Sam to peek outside. The flashlight beam revealed her once-manicured lawn littered with branches, roof shingles, and someone's garden gnome. The rose garden was flattened. Through breaks in the clouds, moonlight illuminated the neighborhood below, which had transformed into a totally alien landscape.

Then the back side of the tropical storm slammed into them with renewed fury.

By dawn, the worst had passed, leaving an eerie silence in its wake and persistent rain. Sam, who had finally dozed off on the hallway floor with Arlo curled against her chest, awoke to sunlight filtering through the windows.

Her phone was fully charged thanks to the generator, but there was no signal. And she'd long given up on having a landline, which seemed to be a magnet for spammers and scammers. Now she was having second thoughts about having jettisoned the landline.

Sam walked into the bathroom and turned the faucet. The water came out slowly, sluggishly, and she grimaced.

Outside, the world was totally transformed. Sam stepped onto her veranda into the drizzle, Arlo keeping close to her heels, and surveyed the damage from her elevated view. Maple Hills looked like a war zone. Massive oaks that had stood for a century were uprooted, some crushing rooftops. The road leading down from her house had disappeared under a sea of mud and debris. Power lines dangled like broken spider webs. In the distance, she could see the historic hotel's distinctive cupola had lost a chunk of its roof.

"Well, this is going to take more than a committee meeting or two to fix," she muttered to herself.

Chapter Two

Arlo's ears perked up at the sound of movement. A figure was picking its way up her driveway through the light rain, carefully navigating around the fallen branches. Sam recognized Alfred's sturdy frame, his beard now flecked with mud and what looked like bits of leaves.

"Alfred!" she called, pushing aside a fallen branch. "Are you and Mandy okay?"

Alfred Jones trudged up her driveway, his burly frame, and gruff, bearded appearance belying his gentle nature. As one of the first neighbors who had welcomed Sam to Maple Hills, Alfred and his wife Mandy had quickly become trusted friends, despite their modest means compared to other residents in the upscale subdivision.

"We're fine," he said, out of breath by the time he reached her. He wiped his brow with a handkerchief. "The house took some damage, but most people's did. Fixing everything's going to take some time."

"You're bleeding," Sam pointed out.

Alfred touched his forehead. "Just a scratch. A branch caught me while I was clearing our driveway." He smiled, though

Sam could see the exhaustion behind it. "Mandy sent me to check on you. She's over on Cedar Lane, helping out the seniors. Mrs. Fitzpatrick's oxygen concentrator needs power, and the Hendersons need help boarding up their broken windows."

Sam nodded, mentally adding these items to her growing task list.

"I've got the generator running," she said. "Tell Mandy she can bring anyone here who needs electricity for medical devices."

Arlo appeared at the door, his tail cautiously wagging as he surveyed the storm damage.

"Hey there, little fella," Alfred said, his voice softening as he scratched behind Arlo's ears. "You weathering the storm okay?"

"He spent most of it under my bed," Sam admitted. "But he's been following me room to room since it passed, like he's doing a damage assessment."

The sound of determined footsteps made them both turn. Nora Snodwick was marching up the hill toward them, her wizened face set in its usual expression of dissatisfaction. The elderly woman had appointed herself the neighborhood's unofficial overseer and critic-in-chief, though Sam had come to recognize a good heart beneath her prickly exterior. Beside her trotted Precious, her beloved pit bull, sporting what appeared to be a custom-made canine rain slicker in bright yellow that matched Nora's own raincoat.

"Your generator's running," Nora announced without preamble. "The only one on the block, I see." Despite her customary abruptness, Sam detected the slightest hint of relief in her eyes.

Sam recognized this as Nora-speak for "I'm checking if you're alive but don't want to admit I was worried."

"Did you walk all the way from your house?" Sam asked, noticing the mud caking Nora's sensible boots.

"Of course I did," Nora sniffed. "My car is trapped in the garage. A tree decided to make itself comfortable across my driveway." She glanced around Sam's property with critical eyes. "You seem to have escaped the worst of it. The Johnsons' roof is half gone, and the Walters' big oak crashed right through their sunroom."

Sam noticed how Nora's hands trembled slightly, despite her brusque demeanor. The storm had clearly rattled her more than she wanted to admit.

"Come inside, both of you," Sam said. "The coffee's hot, and I've got the emergency radio set up in the kitchen."

Arlo greeted Precious with an enthusiastic tail wag. The pit bull in his yellow slicker responded with dignified restraint, though his tail gave a single measured thump.

"Nice to see someone was prepared," Nora remarked, eyeing the organized emergency supplies that Sam had arranged on the kitchen counter. There were flashlights with fresh batteries, a first aid kit, bottled water, and non-perishable food.

"I made a hurricane prep list," Sam explained, pouring coffee into mugs. "Three lists, actually. One for supplies, one for home preparation, and one for emergency contacts." She handed them each a steaming cup.

Alfred wrapped his weathered hands around the mug gratefully. "That's our Sam. Always ready for anything."

"The HOA should have required everyone to have a generator," Nora declared, accepting her coffee with a nod of thanks. "I'm going to bring that up at the next meeting, assuming we ever have one again."

Sam smiled despite herself. Being HOA president had its challenges, especially with residents like Nora, but her predictable crankiness was oddly comforting amid the chaos.

"The radio said the main road is blocked by downed power lines," Sam reported, gesturing to the battery-powered emergency radio on the counter. "They're estimating at least three days before power is restored to our area. But nobody really knows for sure."

They chatted for a few minutes before Alfred said he needed to be on his way. Arlo trailed him to the door, then returned to sit beside Sam, leaning slightly against her leg like he knew she felt uneasy.

Nora remained at the kitchen table, her sharp eyes taking in Sam's expression. "You know," she said with unusual gentleness, "you can't control a hurricane with a checklist."

Sam looked at her in surprise. "I know that," she replied automatically.

"Do you?" Nora raised an eyebrow. "Because that look on your face says you're still trying to organize your way out of this disaster."

Before Sam could respond, there was a sharp knock at the door. Sam hurried to open it, finding Olivia Stanton on her doorstep, drenched despite her raincoat.

"Sorry to just show up," Olivia said, brushing wet hair from her face. "I tried calling but the cell towers must be down."

"What's wrong?" Sam asked, ushering her inside.

Olivia's expression was grim. "The food pantry freezers don't have power. Everything's going to spoil if we don't do something soon. And, for some reason, my own generator isn't working. I could hear yours running, though, Sam."

Nora had risen from her seat, suddenly all business. "Well then, we'd better make space in your freezer for some of the food, hadn't we?" She stood up, her momentary softness replaced by her usual efficiency. "And you might want to make more coffee. Something tells me this is just the beginning."

As if to punctuate Nora's words, the wind picked up again outside, rattling the windows.

Sam was about to respond when another knock came at the door. She opened it to find Lisa Smith, Franklin's mother, looking frazzled with her son standing solemnly beside her. Franklin's perpetually untamed sandy hair was even more disheveled than usual. His eyes lit up at the sight of Arlo.

"Sam, I'm so sorry to barge in like this," Lisa said, her voice strained. "Our roof partially collapsed during the night. We've been at the emergency shelter since 3 AM, but now they're calling in all medical personnel." She rubbed her reddened eyes. "I'm one of the few nurses who can actually get to the hospital, and they're setting up a triage center for storm injuries. Kevin Zhang said he'd pick up Franklin in a couple of hours, but I can't take him to the triage center."

"Of course he can stay here," Sam said without hesitation. She knew Lisa and her husband had gone through a divorce within the last year and figured Lisa didn't want to reach out to her ex.

"You're a lifesaver. Kevin's checking on property damage but said he'd come by as soon as he can. His daughter Emma is with her grandmother on the other side of town."

Franklin stepped inside, still quiet but visibly relieved to see Arlo trotting over to greet him.

"We've got plenty of food and the generator's running," Sam assured Lisa. "He'll be fine here."

"Thank you." Lisa squeezed her son's shoulder. "Be good for Miss Sam, okay? I'll be back as soon as I can."

After Lisa hurried back to her car, Sam turned to find Franklin already on the floor with Arlo, the boy's worries momentarily forgotten as he stroked the dog's soft fur.

"Hungry?" Sam asked.

Franklin nodded. "A little."

"Would you like a peanut butter sandwich?" Sam surprised herself by the question. Usually, she'd come up with an elaborate, healthy, and sustaining meal for any unexpected visitors. But somehow, simple felt better right now.

"Yes, please," the boy said, his voice small but less tense than before.

While Sam prepared the simple lunch, Nora took charge of keeping Franklin occupied, surprisingly gentle as she asked about his experience during the storm. Olivia disappeared into the kitchen to take inventory of the freezer space, her practical nature asserting itself despite the crisis.

An hour later, as Franklin and Arlo dozed together on the living room rug, another vehicle could be heard struggling up the debris-strewn driveway. Nora, who had appointed herself sentinel at the front window, announced, "It's Kevin Zhang's car." Nora, naturally, knew what everyone in the neighborhood drove. She perched at her front window as an unofficial sentry for the Maple Hills subdivision.

Sam looked outside to see a mud-splattered Pathfinder attempting to navigate around fallen branches. Kevin emerged, looking nothing like his usual impeccable self. His designer clothes were rumpled, his short black hair disheveled, and his expression tense as he made his way to the door.

"Kevin," Sam greeted him, opening the door before he could knock. "Everything's good. Franklin's taking a nap with Arlo."

Kevin gave her a smile. "Thanks for watching him for Lisa. I'm sure the hospital has got to be overwhelmed with injuries right now." He ran a hand through his hair, a gesture Sam had never seen from the normally composed businessman. "Everything is a mess."

Sam felt a prickle of unease at his tone. "You mean besides the storm damage?"

Kevin glanced past her to where Nora and Olivia were listening intently. "There's been significant damage at the historic Ridgeview House hotel," he reported, voice low. "Harrison Blackwood's car is there, but no one can reach him."

"The developer?" Olivia asked, stepping forward.

Kevin nodded grimly. "I was assessing storm damage for insurance purposes when I noticed Harrison's car at the hotel. His key fob was inside, but there's no sign of him anywhere."

Sam frowned. "When was the last time anyone saw him?"

"The hotel staff said he insisted on staying overnight to monitor the building damage," Kevin replied, running a hand through his disheveled hair. "Nobody has seen him since last night, and with the cell towers down, there's no way to reach him."

"That doesn't sound good," Sam said, her mind already organizing the information into categories of concern. "Have you contacted emergency services?"

"I tried, but they're overwhelmed with storm response," Kevin said. "With roads blocked and buildings damaged throughout town, a missing person isn't their highest priority right now."

"We should go look for him," Sam decided. Her first thought was of Franklin, but as if reading her mind, Nora spoke up.

"I'll stay with the boy," she said firmly. "Precious and Arlo will keep him company. You two go see what's happened to that developer fellow."

Sam hesitated, her protective instincts warring with her sense of duty.

"I could use your eye for detail," Kevin added. "You notice things others miss. I'll let Lisa know about the change of babysitter."

After a moment's consideration, Sam nodded. "Olivia, can you handle the food bank situation for now?"

"Already on it," Olivia assured her. "I might try to scrounge up a chest freezer and plug it in here to hold more food. Is that okay?"

"Absolutely. I hate that we're going to lose some of that fresh food, though. Maybe somebody at the community center can set something up. I've been watching a few of the town hall meetings online, and they've mentioned having portable generators before. They might have more room for food storage."

"Good idea. I'll try to drive out there and see if I can get something set up with them."

Sam nodded. "Just be careful driving. It sounds like the roads are a mess. Hopefully, cell service will be restored sometime soon." She grabbed her emergency kit and her heavy-duty flashlight. "Let's go."

"Thanks for coming with me," Kevin said, navigating his car around a fallen branch. "I know you've got your hands full."

As the Pathfinder jolted over debris, Sam said, "So what's your connection to Harrison Blackwood? I know you mentioned insurance documentation."

"Well, it's complicated." Kevin kept his eyes on the road, swerving around a fallen mailbox. He sighed, glancing at her. "I handle risk assessment now, but Harrison and I go way back." He paused, hands gripping the steering wheel more firmly. "We were partners on a development in Charlotte a few years ago."

"I take it that didn't go well," Sam said, noting the tension in his shoulders.

"You could say that." Kevin gave a humorless laugh. "I spent months setting everything up with permits, contractors, investors, the works. Then one day, I found myself on the outside looking in." His voice held a bitterness that seemed to surprise even him. "Classic Harrison. He waited until I'd done all the groundwork, then cut me out completely."

"That's awful," Sam said.

Kevin shrugged, though the casual gesture didn't match his expression. "When Harrison showed up here buying up historic properties, I made sure my company got the insurance contract." He glanced at Sam with a hint of satisfaction. "I figured someone should keep an eye on him."

Sam nodded. "He approached me about buying my property. Harrison said my acreage would be perfect for twenty smaller homes."

"Let me guess. When you turned him down, he suggested you might 'work something out'?"

Sam raised an eyebrow. "His exact words, actually."

"That's Harrison," Kevin said grimly. "Some people never change."

The Pathfinder slowed as they approached the Ridgeview House hotel. The historic building had weathered many storms in its long existence, but Sam could see significant damage to the east wing. Sections of the slate roof had been torn away, and part of the ornate widow's walk was missing.

"That's his car," Kevin said, pointing to a flashy red Pathfinder parked haphazardly at the entrance.

As they pulled up, a young woman in a hotel uniform hurried out, her dark hair escaping from what might earlier have been a neat bun. Her face was pale.

"Mr. Zhang? Were you able to find him?" The woman glanced over at Sam. "I'm Maya Lopez, the assistant manager."

"No, but we're going to look around the property since his car's here," Kevin said. "It seems pretty unlikely that somebody would have picked him up last night with the storm raging like it was."

Maya wrapped her arms around herself. "I'll walk with you. I'm worried something might have happened to Mr. Blackwood. He wasn't being very careful with the storm."

"When did you last see him?" Sam asked.

"Around eight last night, when the storm was at its worst. He was heading to check the east wing. We told him it wasn't safe, but he wouldn't listen." Maya shivered, whether from nerves or from the wind still whipping up, it was hard to say. "We've been trying to find him, but with half the staff unable to get here and the power out, we haven't made much progress."

"Let's check the east wing," Sam suggested.

They followed Maya through the grand lobby, where water had pooled on the marble floors. Emergency lighting cast long shadows as they made their way down a corridor.

"We've checked most of the rooms," Maya said, "but there's debris blocking the conservatory. It connects to the east wing."

As they approached, Sam noticed a door hanging ajar. Maya pushed it wider, and they entered what had once been a beautiful glass-enclosed space. Several windows had shattered, and branches from a fallen tree had punched through the roof.

"Be careful," Kevin warned, stepping over a fallen beam.

The conservatory opened onto an east-facing terrace. Sam stepped carefully onto the stone surface, mindful of slick puddles.

That's when she saw him.

Harrison Blackwood lay sprawled near a pile of branches and roof debris, his expensive clothes soaked through, designer sneakers coated in mud. His salt-and-pepper hair was matted against his head, and his shattered phone lay nearby.

"No," Maya said softly.

Chapter Three

Kevin moved forward, but Sam caught his arm.

"Wait," she said quietly. "Something's not right."

While Maya fumbled with her radio, Sam's eyes cataloged inconsistencies. The debris around Blackwood looked arranged rather than randomly fallen. And there was a dark stain on his clothing. She studied the dark stains more carefully. They weren't typical mud or water stains from the storm. Instead, they formed distinctive patterns—metallic gray with unusual bluish-white edges, almost like rust but with a different coloration.

"What is it?" Kevin asked in a low voice.

"The debris sort of looks staged," Sam murmured. "And those marks on his clothing are odd."

Maya's voice cut through the moment. "Phil! East terrace, quickly. We found Mr. Blackwood. He didn't make it."

As Maya turned back to them, Sam continued studying the scene. Something about the roofline of the east wing caught her eye. It was an asymmetry that hadn't been there before, some kind of missing element she couldn't immediately pinpoint but knew should be there.

Kevin stepped closer. "This wasn't an accident, was it?"

"We should call the police," said Sam. She was already pulling out her phone before she realized it had no signal.

Maya shook her head. "The cell tower must be down. Let me tell Phil to go to the police station instead of joining me here." She quickly radioed him. Phil didn't sound delighted to be heading out to find the police, but tersely accepted the assignment.

Phil must have done a fairly good job either picking his way down the debris-strewn roads by car, or by walking to the station. In thirty minutes, the police had arrived. Considering the magnitude of the issues the storm had caused, Sam guessed that it was Harrison's local prominence that had spurred them to interrupt what they were doing to get to the hotel.

Sam had met the police chief before, at a local fundraising event she'd attended. Bill Hawkins was in his late-fifties with a stocky build, his uniform shirt already showing sweat stains despite the early hour. Sam noticed the dark circles under his eyes and figured he hadn't slept since the storm hit.

"Well," he said, surveying the scene with a grim expression. "This is not how I hoped to start the day." He nodded toward Sam and Kevin. "Either of you touch anything?"

"No," Sam replied. "We found him just like this."

Chief Hawkins crouched beside Harrison's body, his knees cracking audibly. He studied the scene without handling anything, then looked up at the damaged roof, his eyes narrowing.

"Maya tells me you two were looking for him," he said, rising slowly.

Kevin nodded. "I noticed his car was still in the parking lot with the key fob inside, which seemed weird. When no one had seen him since last night, I was concerned, especially with all the storm damage."

Officer Martinez, who looked to be in her early thirties, approached with a notebook. Unlike the chief, her uniform was still crisp, though her eyes reflected the same exhaustion. She greeted the chief.

Sam pointed to the strange marks on Harrison's clothing. "Those stains don't look like typical mud or water from the storm."

Chief Hawkins followed her gaze, studying the distinctive patterns—metallic gray with unusual bluish-white edges. He looked at Sam more carefully. "You're right. What made you notice that?"

"I'm detail-oriented," Sam said with a slight shrug. "And the debris around him looks almost arranged, doesn't it? Not like it fell naturally."

The chief's eyebrows rose slightly. He turned to Officer Martinez. "Make a note of that. We'll need photos of those stains before the medical examiner moves him."

"Yes, sir," she replied, jotting in her notebook.

Hawkins turned back to Sam. "You've got a good eye." His expression turned more serious. "I also hear you had some history with Mr. Blackwood."

Sam felt her stomach tighten. "History might be overstating it. He wanted to buy my property for development. I declined."

"And how did he take that?" Hawkins asked, watching her face.

"Not well," Sam admitted. "Apparently, he wasn't used to hearing 'no.'"

The chief nodded slowly. "Did anyone else in town have problems with him that you two know of?"

"Several people," Kevin said. "Harrison wasn't making a lot of friends with his development plans."

Hawkins turned to Kevin. "I feel like we've met before, but I can't remember your name."

"Kevin Zhang. I'm handling the insurance documentation for his properties." Kevin hesitated. "We were also former business partners."

"Former?" The chief's attention sharpened. "It sounds like there's a story there."

"There is," Kevin acknowledged. "But not one that ends with me killing him."

Chief Hawkins's radio crackled, and a very staticky transmission came through. It was difficult to understand the voice, but the urgency was clear.

"Chief? We've got—." The transmission cut out. Then they could hear part of another sentence. "Landslide. Multiple vehicles trapped." More interference. Then "—need backup right away."

"Copy that," Bill said quickly. He turned to Officer Martinez. "I need you to secure the scene here. And get photos of everything, especially those stains Ms. Prescott noticed. Treat it like a crime scene, just in case. I'll send the ME when they can get through."

"You'll get statements from us later?" Sam asked.

Hawkins nodded. "I'll want detailed statements from both of you once we handle this emergency." He fixed them with a significant look. "Don't leave town."

"In this weather? Not likely," Kevin said dryly.

"I'll need to borrow your vehicle," the chief said to Kevin. "My officer took our only functioning cruiser."

"Of course," Kevin said. "I can take you wherever you need to go. Is the landslide serious?"

"Everything's serious right now," Hawkins replied wearily. "The whole county's underwater or sliding downhill." He looked back at Harrison's body. "But that doesn't mean we can ignore what happened here."

The wind kicked up again, blowing more debris down from the trees overhead. Kevin hesitated. "Why don't you wait inside the hotel?" he asked Sam. "I'll drive you back home as soon as I can."

"You know, I think I'll go over to the bookstore right down the street. I thought I saw Charlotte's car there when we drove by. I'll check in with her and see how her shop fared," said Sam.

As she turned to leave, she cast one last glance at the hotel's east wing roofline. Something was missing that should have been there—she just couldn't put her finger on what.

Chapter Four

The downtown area of Sunset Ridge was virtually unrecognizable. What had been charming historic streets lined with small businesses now resembled a war zone. Massive trees, some hundreds of years old, had been uprooted, crashing through storefronts and blocking entire sections of Main Street. The floodwaters had receded a little but had left behind a thick layer of mud that was coating everything.

A group of volunteers waded through ankle-deep water at the intersection, trying to clear a storm drain. In front of the hardware store, the owner was already boarding up shattered windows while neighbors helped salvage what inventory they could. The historic gazebo in the town square had lost its roof entirely, and park benches had been carried halfway down the block by the force of the water.

The town's distinctive clock tower still stood, but its face was smashed, the hands frozen at what must have been the moment the power failed. Downed power lines draped across roads, while transformers lay twisted and broken on the wet ground. Every few feet, Sam had to navigate around debris.

There were shingles, siding, branches, and pieces of buildings that had broken free in the wind.

Near the intersection, a sinkhole had opened up, swallowing half the street. Orange cones had been placed around it. The rushing water had carved new channels through town, exposing pipes and undercutting foundations. Several buildings showed ominous cracks along their facades. A chill went down Sam's spine at the damage. It made her wonder how many lives were lost to the storm.

As Sam approached Twice-Told Tales, Charlotte's bookstore, she saw water had reached at least three feet up the walls, leaving a distinct line of mud and debris. The front window had a spiderweb of cracks but somehow remained intact. The shop's hanging sign swung precariously from a single chain, creaking in the wind.

The bell above the door gave a weak, exhausted-sounding jingle as Sam pushed it open. Inside, Charlotte Webb looked up from where she was frantically moving books to higher shelves. Her petite frame was dwarfed by the stacks of volumes surrounding her. Dark brown hair escaped from its usual messy bun, and her wire-rimmed reading glasses sat askew on her nose. Ink stained her fingers, and her jeans were splattered with mud up to the knees. Despite the chaos, her grandmother's cameo pin was still fastened securely at the collar of her long-sleeved top.

"Hey, Sam." Charlotte's tired face brightened momentarily. "Glad you're okay." She pushed her glasses up and climbed down from the small step ladder she'd been using. "Why are you downtown? It's not really safe to be out." She made a face. "Aside from business owners trying to make inroads with the debris that was left behind."

Sam closed the door behind her, taking in the damage. Water had clearly surged through the shop, leaving a muddy line about three feet up the walls. Books had been hastily stacked on tables and counters, and a small generator hummed in the corner, powering a dehumidifier and a single lamp.

"I'm so sorry about this. Have you been able to gauge how much you've lost?"

Charlotte sighed. "It's a lot, but I don't think it's going to force me to close. At least, I really hope not. With a name like Charlotte Webb, what else could I possibly do with my life besides run a bookstore?"

Sam gave her a quick hug. "I love your store. I'm glad to hear you're not going to have to shut down."

"I love it, too. But you still haven't answered my question about what you're doing downtown."

"I was just up at the Ridgeview with Kevin Zhang," Sam said, carefully choosing her words. "There's been an incident involving Harrison Blackwood."

Charlotte's expression changed subtly. "Harrison? What's he done now?"

Sam recalled again the tension she'd noticed between Charlotte and Harrison at the last town meeting. The developer had made no secret of his desire to acquire the block where Twice-Told Tales stood, and Charlotte had been one of the most vocal opponents of his plans.

"Actually," Sam said, moving closer and lowering her voice, "he's dead. They found his body at the hotel."

Charlotte pressed her lips together tightly. "Sorry to hear that. I have the feeling we're going to hear about a lot more people who've lost their lives to this storm."

Sam decided not to tell her the death seemed suspicious. Charlotte might be more willing to offer truthful opinions without knowing Harrison might have been murdered. "Can I give you a hand?" she asked. "I see you brought in boxes. Do you want me to box some books for you?"

Her offer had the unintended effect of making Charlotte burst into tears. "Sorry. This is a lot for me. Yes, boxing books would be amazing. Although I'm not sure where I'm going to put them. My house is already crammed full of stuff."

"I can take them to my place," offered Sam. "It's climate-controlled because I have a generator running."

"Would you? It wouldn't be for too long, I promise. Just until I can get the shop dried out. And you wouldn't need to take *everything*, either—just the most valuable books. I've got collector's items that I really want to get out of here."

"Of course," Sam said. "Just point them out to me, and I'll get started."

A couple of minutes later, Sam was methodically packing books into boxes. Charlotte glanced over at her. "Harrison wasn't out in the storm, was he? I was just wondering what happened to him."

Sam said carefully, "He was outside. I'm not sure why."

"I bet there are going to be plenty of people who are found in their cars," said Charlotte somberly. "Trying to get out of the storm's path." She paused. "I do feel bad for him, but I wasn't his number one fan."

Sam said, "I totally understand that. He and I didn't see eye-to-eye, either."

"Really? He wasn't trying to buy your property, was he? That seems to have been his modus operandi."

"He was," said Sam. "All of it. He wanted to knock down my house and put up a ton of others."

Charlotte gave a short laugh. "Somehow, that doesn't surprise me. That guy was unbelievable. I mean, you live in a historic home. I don't think the town would let him knock that house down even if you'd sold it to him."

"True. But I wasn't going to. He was wanting to buy your shop, wasn't he?"

Charlotte said, "Not just mine. Everybody's business on the block. I don't want to say bad things about the dead, but he was a real piece of work. He could get nasty if he didn't get his way. And he wasn't getting his way with the business owners."

Sam nodded. "Yeah. He was badmouthing me around town. At least, that's what people were telling me. He wasn't happy I turned down his offer." She was certain Hawkins, the police chief, was going to be coming back around to speak with her again when he found out how acrimonious her conversations with Harrison Blackwood had been. Sam was sure Harrison had been murdered. It made her want to do as much as she could to find out who else got on his bad side.

Charlotte shook her head. "Harrison just liked getting his own way, I guess. I'm sorry about what happened to him, though. This storm was something else."

"You hunkered down at home, right? You weren't out trying to check on your shop?"

Charlotte said, "Are you kidding? That storm scared me to death. We're not used to that kind of weather here. How could a hurricane end up coming through the Appalachians? I mean, I guess it had been downgraded to a tropical storm, but it sure didn't feel like it. I didn't show up here at the shop until about an hour ago." She ran a hand through her hair. "I didn't sleep a wink. All I could think about were my books. I was kicking myself for not preparing more. I should have gotten the books out of here yesterday and just stacked them in my hall at home or something."

"Don't beat yourself up about it. The forecasters had no idea the storm was going to be like this, remember? They were telling us to just expect a lot of rain and maybe some power outages with downed limbs. Nobody said it was going to be like this. We don't usually *get* hurricanes in the mountains."

Charlotte said, "True. I wasn't being totally slack." She sighed, looking around at the mess in her bookstore. "This is going to take a while to get cleaned up. But then, I guess book shopping isn't going to be anyone's priority in the next few weeks. Everyone is going to be focused on cleaning up their own property damage."

Sam wanted to move the conversation back to Harrison. "Thinking back to Harrison. Was there anybody else who was upset with him? Besides you and me, I mean?"

Charlotte gave her a curious look, but said, "Sure. You're not feeling guilty about getting Harrison mad, are you? You didn't know he was going to die. And you and I were hardly alone in our dislike for the guy. You remember Diane Foster?"

"She's in the agility club with me. Isn't she some sort of environmental worker? Or activist?"

"You got it. She was an environmental lawyer who quit to focus on local causes. Anyway, she discovered a rare bat species living in the attics of a building Harrison planned on demolishing. She was *livid* when he tried to cover up an environmental impact study."

Sam said slowly, "I think there was something in the local paper about it. Doesn't Diane's father run that little nature center on the edge of town?"

"Exactly. As a matter of fact, it was going to lose its parking access under Harrison's development plans. Anyway, she clearly wasn't happy with Harrison, either. She was monitoring the bats to get endangered species protection. I was at the town hall meeting last month when Diane confronted Harrison. It got pretty heated."

Sam finished packing two boxes and turned to ask Charlotte what else needed to be put away. She noticed Charlotte's hand was bleeding through a small bandage. "Are you okay? Your hand is bleeding."

Charlotte tucked her hand into her folded arm. "It's nothing. Just got cut on some glass here. I put a bandage on it, but it keeps reopening because I'm using it."

Sam glanced up from the box she'd just finished. "Anything else you need me to box up?"

Charlotte peered around the shop, an exhausted expression on her face. "Besides the collector's items, the local and regional books would be the hardest to replace, if you want to box those. I really appreciate the help."

"It's no trouble. I'm waiting on a ride back home, so I've got time to kill while I wait."

Charlotte pushed mud out of the corner of the shop with her mop. "Thinking back on Harrison, I can also name Victor Reid as someone who wasn't happy with him."

"Sounds like Harrison got on the bad side of half the town," said Sam. "I don't think I know Victor."

"He's a tall, lanky guy. He usually wears tweed jackets with elbow patches."

Sam said, "Is he a professor? With clothes like that, I can't imagine what else he'd do."

"Former professor, yes. He lost his university position recently."

Sam said slowly, "Why would he have clashed with Harrison?"

"Oh, he's an architectural historian. He's been fighting to preserve historic buildings." Charlotte grinned at her. "Victor would have totally been in your corner about your house. It's from the late-1800s, isn't it?"

"That's right. He sounds like a good friend to have in case another developer tries to do the same thing." Sam paused. "What about other local businesses? I'm sure you weren't the only one wanting to protect your shop."

"Trevor Mills," Charlotte said immediately. "He's a third-generation contractor who specializes in historic renovation. Harrison awarded a major renovation bid to an out-of-state company, even though I hear Trevor's bid was better. Trevor's been struggling ever since. Apparently, he'd invested in equipment specifically for the project."

Sam said slowly, "I know Trevor. His daughter walks Arlo for me sometimes."

"He's a nice guy. And a great contractor, I hear."

Sam said, "Sure sounds like a lot of folks wanted Harrison gone."

"When you bulldoze through a town like Harrison was doing, you tend to make enemies." Charlotte held up her hands. "But I'm sorry he's dead, like I said." She frowned. "So it really was a storm-related death? Because there were so many people who didn't like him."

"I'm sure we'll find out later if it wasn't," said Sam.

"Well, I was at home, sleepless, with my cat and a bottle of merlot, waiting for my roof to blow off," she said with a short laugh. "No witnesses, I'm afraid."

Kevin pushed open the door of the bookstore. "Sam?"

"Hey there, Kevin." Sam turned to Charlotte. "I'd better run." She picked up one of the boxes, and Kevin grabbed a couple more.

"Thanks so much for getting those books out of here, Sam," said Charlotte. "I promise I'll be by to pick them back up soon."

Chapter Five

A couple of minutes later, Kevin pulled his Pathfinder carefully around a fallen branch in the road. The windshield wipers worked overtime against the persistent drizzle.

"Thanks for driving me," Sam said, glad not to be navigating the roads herself. "I should go back and check on Franklin and Arlo."

Kevin nodded, his eyes fixed on the road. "I need to get to my mom's and check on Emma, myself."

They fell into silence as they approached the section of road where the mudslide had occurred earlier. County workers had cleared just enough space for one vehicle to pass. Kevin slowed to a crawl, easing past the mountain of mud and tree roots that had slid down the hillside.

"Mother Nature's quite the developer herself," Kevin remarked, gesturing toward the altered landscape. "She reshapes everything overnight without even asking permission."

"At least she doesn't buy up historic buildings just to tear them down," Sam replied dryly, still thinking about Harrison.

Kevin's grip tightened slightly on the steering wheel. "Or push out local businesses for a quick profit."

An uncomfortable silence settled between them. Sam sensed there was more Kevin wanted to say.

"Those marks on Harrison's clothes," Kevin finally said, his voice low. "Did they look familiar to you?"

Sam considered her words carefully. "Not really. Just enough to know they didn't match typical storm debris."

"It was zinc oxidation, I think," Kevin said, his professional demeanor returning. "From my restoration documentation work, I can tell you it leaves distinctive stains—metallic gray with bluish-white edges. Specifically, the kind used on the hotel's roofline ornaments."

"You think Harrison was up on the roof? What—and fell?" Sam was already thinking that his injuries should have been more evident after a fall from the roof.

"I'm not sure," admitted Kevin. "It's just sort of weird. Of course, he shouldn't have been up on the roof in that kind of weather."

"With Harrison gone, what happens to his development company?" she asked.

"I'm not really sure," said Kevin again.

Before she could respond, Kevin changed the subject.

"How's your generator holding up? I heard your house is the only one around with power. I guess it's hooked up to your natural gas line."

"It is, yes. It's running well so far. I'll need to check the oil when I get back, though."

A few minutes later, Kevin pulled up into Sam's formidable driveway. Although she protested, he insisted on driving her all the way up to the top, since the rain had picked up. Then he helped carry in the books from Charlotte's bookstore, putting them right inside her door. She thanked him, advised him to turn around instead of trying to tackle her driveway in reverse, and headed inside.

She found Franklin and Nora sitting at the kitchen table, coloring on printer paper. Since Sam's house wasn't particularly outfitted for children, they were coloring with pencils. She supposed that meant they were technically sketching, not coloring.

Arlo joyfully bounded up to greet her, wearing a small bandana he hadn't had on when she'd left, and she stooped down to give him a cuddle. She was starting to feel like she needed a cuddle, herself.

"How is everything going?" asked Sam as cheerfully as she could. No reason to worry Franklin with too much gloom and doom. His world had been disrupted enough in the last twenty-four hours.

"We're having a wonderful time," said Nora firmly, giving Sam a warning look as if to tell her she didn't need to talk much about the storm or anything else troubling.

"We sorted batteries by size," offered Franklin, who seemed entirely too pleased by this rather unfun activity.

"I believed a bit of structure might be in order," said Nora.

"And I thought *I* was organized," said Sam with a rueful smile. "Well, thanks very much. I'll do my best to preserve your system."

"Various neighbors came by and wanted to know if there was any sort of emergency response for the neighborhood. Response by the HOA, I assumed."

Franklin said in a chipper voice, "Miss Nora had me make a list of the visitors. She said I had excellent penmanship."

Sam asked, "Did Arlo and Precious have fun?" She noticed Precious was now wearing one of Sam's ancient tank tops. Precious gave her a smug grin, baring his teeth as he did.

"Indeed they did. Franklin and I gave them both basic disaster training," said Nora, as if this were perfectly normal. "They can now fetch specific items from your emergency kit."

"Can they now?" Sam glanced over at Arlo, who wagged his tail innocently.

"Well, Arlo can," admitted Nora. "Precious prefers to supervise."

As if on cue, Precious lifted his blocky head. The pit bull gave what could only be described as a dignified sniff, then settled back down again, eyes still watching the proceedings with what appeared to be managerial interest.

Nora gave Sam a curious look. If Franklin hadn't been there, Nora would have been pumping her relentlessly for information.

Sam said, "Franklin, while you're sketching, I'm going to borrow Miss Nora for a second."

"Sure," said Franklin without looking up from his drawing.

They stepped out onto the terrace. Sam tried to ignore the many limbs and the few trees that were downed on her property. Nothing was going to be perfect for a while and the sooner she faced that fact, the better-off she'd be.

Nora launched right into the interrogation. "What happened to that developer?"

Sam was surprised that Nora knew who Harrison Blackwood was. But then she realized she shouldn't be. Nora knew just about everything that went on in Sunset Ridge. "He's dead."

"Hmph," said Nora as if the man had been to blame for his own death and possibly the storm, too. "He was no good you know."

"I've heard he could be a difficult man to deal with," said Sam mildly.

Nora peered at Sam through narrowed eyes. "He was over here, too. I saw his fancy car in your driveway, not too long ago. I meant to call you about that. I had the horrible feeling you might take the man's offer and sell this house and property. I wouldn't have been able to bear all the noisy construction and the view being destroyed. Who knows what kind of horrors he'd have developed here?"

Sam thought that must have taken Nora a good deal of restraint.

Nora continued, "I guess the storm killed him." She looked shrewdly at Sam for a reaction to her statement.

Sam knew it would be all over town if Nora knew Sam suspected Harrison's death was a homicide. "I suppose so," she said simply. Then, "Tell me more about who came by and what people were saying is needed."

Nora listed a few neighbors' names, then talked about cell service being out, grocery stores closed because of flooding and lack of power, and no way to get cash because of power outages affecting ATMs. Then she said, "And Aiden came by. He seemed very concerned about you."

She gave Sam a penetrating stare. Sam made sure her expression was as bland as possible. The last thing she wanted was for Nora to spread rumors about her and Aiden, a former cop turned high school teacher. Whatever was developing between them was too new to even call a relationship.

Sam said, "Got it. Did you tell him I was fine?"

Nora sniffed again. "I did. Although I didn't really *know* that, did I? That's the worst thing. There's no way for anyone to really communicate with anyone else."

Sam was already thinking about ways to help with communication. "Doesn't Alfred Jones have walkie-talkies?" Then she frowned. "Actually, I have walkie-talkies, myself. I'd forgotten about that. I purchased them for my emergency kit when they went on sale a couple of years ago."

"Oh, good. Those will be useful. And yes, Alfred does have them, and he's not the only one. Franklin has one and his mom the other, he told me. But they just use them in the neighborhood because the range is only a mile or two. What are you thinking?"

Sam said slowly, "I was thinking about setting up a command center at the Maple Ridge clubhouse. We could pool neighborhood supplies of things like portable generators, portable chargers, chainsaws, and things like that. If wi-fi comes back before cell service, charging stations would help folks who need to make phone calls over wi-fi. Maybe even a community pantry might help, since we don't know when the grocery stores will open back up. We could have rotating volunteers for the clubhouse, and I could be on the other end here at the house. If my place is the only one with a functioning generator, people could come to my house to cook things, charge devices, whatever."

Her brain started reaching beyond that, too. The subdivision had a few commons areas for picnics and other activities, and she could only imagine how badly those were hit. She didn't even really know what kind of shape the clubhouse was in. From what Sam could tell, the whole town had taken a major hit. Who knew when tree cutters or landscapers might be able to come by and clear trees and other debris? Some of the homeowners might have chainsaws. They could create a team of volunteers to at least help clear the roads in Maple Hills to make it easier to get to the main road outside the subdivision.

Sam tuned back in to Nora, who was talking forcefully about something to do with her neighborhood friends Mandy and Alfred. "Sorry," said Sam. "What were you saying? Their home was damaged? I saw Alfred this morning, but he didn't tell me things were that bad."

"You know how he downplays things. It's quite a mess, from what I understand. You know they don't have much extra money, and it's all such a pity. To think they were about to award that scholarship next month." She sipped her tea with an air of someone who had just dropped vital intelligence.

"Scholarship?" Sam looked up from her list. "What scholarship?"

Nora looked smug, always glad to know something others didn't. "They've been putting aside money for fifteen years. It started after Alfred's nephew couldn't afford electrician training." Her voice softened slightly. "Every year they've added to it, even when their own roof was leaking. This was finally the year they had enough."

"For a full scholarship?" Sam asked, genuinely impressed.

"For one deserving student from Sunset Ridge to attend a technical college," Nora confirmed. "The selection committee was meeting next month. Alfred and Mandy were finally going to see their dream realized." She shook her head. "Now with their house damaged, I'm guessing they may have to dip into the fund."

Sam felt something twist in her chest. After all those years of sacrifice, to have their generosity derailed by the storm seemed particularly cruel.

"How bad is their house?" Sam asked quietly.

Nora's usual sharp gaze held genuine concern. "Bad enough. But you know Alfred and Mandy—they're too busy helping everyone else to mention their own troubles."

"Thanks for letting me know," said Sam, mentally adding to her growing list of community needs. "Maybe we can figure out a way to help them without them knowing. They'd never accept charity."

Nora nodded approvingly. "Now you're thinking."

Sam glanced at her watch. "In the meantime, I'm going over to the clubhouse to see what kind of shape it's in. I can take Franklin with me."

Nora glared at her. "No you will not. I'm having more fun than I've had in a long time, despite the damage outside. I'll entertain Franklin, thank you very much."

Nora wasn't one for platitudes, so she meant business. And Sam knew better than to stand in her way. "Okay. Just send somebody down to the clubhouse if you need a break. I'm sure folks will be by the house, since the generator is running. And I'll grab the walkie-talkies. You can have one of them here."

Sam explained to Franklin where she was going before she left, mainly so he could choose to come with her if he really wanted to. He'd seemed perfectly content with Nora, but she wasn't sure if he was just an excellent little actor. But he said he'd stay put, that he and Nora hadn't finished their coloring. And that Nora was going to show him how to do a magic trick, a fact that Sam found rather astonishing. She showed Nora how to work the walkie-talkie, then headed out.

Chapter Six

The clubhouse was usually an easy walk from Sam's house. This time, however, it proved more of an adventure as she walked it in light rain. A pine tree lay completely across the road at one point, and the road was strewn with debris, deck chairs, and roofing in other sections. She realized how fortunate she was to live near the entrance of the neighborhood, which hadn't been blocked. It would be good to see if the other entrance was clear or not. It could be that she was one of the few people actually able to drive out of the Maple Hills subdivision, considering there was debris blocking the road just past her house.

She was relieved to see the Maple Hills clubhouse stood firm despite the hurricane. Its brick and wood siding had weathered the storm better than most buildings in the subdivision. The flowerpots that normally hung from the porch had vanished, leaving empty hooks. Rocking chairs were scattered across the lawn or overturned on the porch.

Shingles covered the ground around the building, torn loose from one corner of the roof where a branch had struck but not broken through. The east side gutters hung at odd angles and the clubhouse sign lay face-down in the mud. Wooden stairs remained solid under a layer of wet leaves and debris.

Sam walked inside, using her key. The main room looked almost normal, although the whole space was dimmer than normal with no electricity. The kitchenette stood ready, although its contents were certainly going to need attention at some point soon. Water stains marked a few ceiling tiles, but the roof had held.

The door of the clubhouse swung open, and Sam turned to see Aiden Wood stepping inside with a box of emergency supplies balanced against his hip. His tall frame filled the doorway, and his tousled black hair was still damp from the rain.

"I thought I might find you here," he said, setting the box down. His expression shifted to one of concern as he looked her over. "How are you holding up? When I stopped by your house earlier, Nora said you were fine, but she has her own definition of 'fine.'"

Sam said, "I'm doing okay. The house came through better than most. How about you?"

"Good. A few shingles and one broken window, but nothing major." His voice carried relief. "I'm glad you're fine. With the cell service down, I was worried when I couldn't immediately check on you."

Their eyes met, and Sam felt that familiar flutter she'd been trying to ignore since moving to Sunset Ridge. After Chad, and especially after his arrest, Sam had sworn off relationships entirely. But something about Aiden was different. He'd slowly chipped away at her defenses with his steady presence, always keeping a respectful distance. They'd had conversations at the park, and he'd helped with documentation for her historic home registration. There had been occasional coffees that weren't officially dates but which she thought they'd both really enjoyed. They had something neither of them had named yet, perhaps not wanting to jinx it.

"You got here at the perfect time," she said, gesturing around her. "I'm thinking this can be a command center."

Aiden nodded, immediately understanding her plan without requiring explanation. That was one thing about Aiden—he didn't need everything spelled out. The former detective turned teacher simply got it.

Aiden lowered his voice. "I heard about Harrison Blackwood."

Sam's grip tightened on her clipboard. Of course he'd have heard. Former cops always had connections. "It looked to me like the storm wasn't what killed him," she said in an equally low tone.

"I figured as much when I heard about the state police heading toward the hotel." He unpacked the box systematically, bringing out batteries, flashlights, and first aid supplies. "They're stranded at the north roadblock for now, waiting for crews to clear the road."

"So we're on our own for a while longer," said Sam.

"The county says it's at least forty-eight hours before the main roads are passable." He pulled out a few walkie-talkies. "I have a couple of these from the school." He glanced at the table where Sam had laid hers and quirked an eyebrow. "I should have known you'd have your own."

"Oh, I had some in case of an emergency. Sadly, it appears an emergency has happened."

"I've got a few high school students who live nearby and are ready to help," Aiden said, arranging the walkie-talkies in a precise row. "They need community service hours anyway. If we don't need them for Maple Hills, I can easily get them to other hubs where volunteers are needed."

"What are you seeing out there?" Sam asked, setting the clipboard down to help unpack. "In our subdivision, I mean."

Aiden's face grew serious. "Three houses have significant structural damage. The Andersons' roof collapsed. The Mitchell family spent the night in their car because a tree fell across their bedroom. Five seniors need medication refrigerated. Eight more need power for medical devices."

"Those with medical needs should come to my house," Sam said automatically. "My generator's holding steady."

"I already suggested that. Alfred is driving Mrs. Fitzpatrick over now. The student volunteers are clearing pathways between houses so people can move around more easily."

Their hands brushed as they both reached for the same bundle of emergency blankets. Sam felt that small electric jolt again but kept her expression neutral. This wasn't the time.

"I checked in with Charlotte at the bookstore," Sam said, changing the subject. "She gave me some interesting background on Harrison and his conflicts with locals."

"Anyone in particular?" Aiden arranged the blankets by size.

"Victor Reid, for one. He's the architectural historian. Apparently, he and Harrison had some heated exchanges about preserving the historic district."

Aiden nodded. "Victor is passionate about those old buildings. His office in the old library building is probably flooded. Victor is something of a friend of mine. I'll add it to my check-in rounds."

"Do you mind if I tag along when you do? I'd like to talk with him."

"Are you planning to investigate on your own?" Aiden's tone was careful, concerned but not pressing.

"I'm just gathering information. I was at the scene. The police will want a full statement." She paused. "Frankly, it's not just that. I'm probably a suspect, myself."

Aiden frowned. "Really? Why would you say that?"

"It sounds like you're one of the few who don't know that Harrison approached me about selling my house."

Aiden gave her a weary look. "Oh, boy. I'm guessing he didn't want to preserve your house, either. He wanted to knock it down and put up a ton of shoddy houses in its place."

"That's about right. Anyway, he didn't take kindly to the fact that I turned him down. A few people told me at the time that he was badmouthing me around town."

Aiden narrowed his eyes, and Sam quickly added, "Hey, it was no skin off my nose. Harrison was obviously not a good sport about losing. Anyway, the cops will likely see that as a motive. I'd like the murder to be solved for that reason. It would nice if my name was cleared."

Aiden nodded. "Got it." He hesitated. "Sam, be careful who you talk to. If it wasn't the storm that killed Harrison, then there's somebody dangerous out there."

"I know." She caught his gaze. "I'm just going to listen."

"Got it. And, of course, feel free to meet up with me tomorrow to see Victor. He's temporarily living at the old library building; the one that's vacant. Well, vacant except for Victor," said Aiden.

"Okay. Is he staying there because of work? Is he researching the building or something?"

Aiden said, "Partly that, but partly he's there because he was let go from his teaching job at the university. The town is letting Victor stay there while he's researching the history and trying to come up with a case for preserving the building. Of course, that was when Harrison was eyeing the property. Maybe it's not as urgent now for him to research."

The clubhouse door opened as Mandy Jones hurried in, her curly hair tied back in a bandana. "Oh, thank goodness. People are saying this is headquarters now? Mrs. Peterson's insulin needs refrigeration, and the Walkers need help moving a tree that's blocking their front door."

"I've got the Walkers," Aiden said, already picking up his jacket.

Sam said, "I can show Mrs. Peterson to my house. And Mandy, can you start a list of who has what supplies they're willing to share? Chainsaws, generators, water purification tablets—anything useful."

By late afternoon, Sam had transformed the clubhouse into a functioning command center. She'd used the large whiteboard from the clubhouse office to create a neighborhood map, marking affected homes, resources, and volunteer assignments.

Sam glanced at the wall where she'd mounted a large map of the town, showing damaged areas, road closures, and resource centers.

"Honestly, Samantha, why can't you just go with the flow like normal kids?"

Her mother's voice echoed from the past, dismissive and irritated as teenage Sam had created yet another schedule to manage the household tasks her parents neglected. Meal planning. Bill payment reminders.

She'd learned early that if she didn't take charge, things fell apart. If she didn't make the dentist appointments, they didn't happen. If she didn't keep track of the electric bill, the lights went out. If she didn't plan the meals, everyone ate cereal for dinner. At least, if there was milk in the fridge. And there were a few times they'd settled on dry cereal.

Taking care of others had become second nature long before she'd created and sold a successful productivity app or taken on the HOA presidency in her subdivision. It was as familiar as breathing.

Some things were beyond planning and organization. But she could manage helping her community weather a crisis.

"We need something more permanent than word-of-mouth," Sam said to Alfred, who'd returned with his toolbox. "Most people don't even know we've set this up."

"I've got some plywood in my truck," Alfred offered, running a hand through his graying beard. "We could make signs for the neighborhood entrances."

Twenty minutes later, Alfred had created two large signs. With Mandy's precise handwriting, they now displayed: *"Maple*

Hills emergency center: clubhouse open 7AM-7PM. Medical needs at Sam's (42 Hillcrest). Walkie-Talkie Channel 3 for assistance."

Sam helped Alfred load the signs into his truck. "How are things going with your house? I hear the damage was pretty extensive."

"Oh, Mandy and I'll manage," said Alfred quickly. He was always one to downplay his own issues, although his finances could be tough. Sam knew he and Mandy must really believe in the scholarship they were planning on sponsoring. They'd had significant money issues before, to the point where Alfred had needed to borrow money. For them not to dip into that fund showed real dedication. She was still mulling over a way to help the two of them out. After all, they were always trying to help others.

By sunset, Sam had established a systematic response plan. The high school volunteers had been assigned to clearing debris, delivering supplies, and checking on elderly residents.

The sun was setting as Sam finally walked back up the hill to her house. Her legs felt like lead, and her back ached from lifting supplies all day. Arlo greeted her at the door, his small body wiggling with joy. He made some of her stress melt away. Behind him, the living room had been transformed into a makeshift medical center, with two elderly neighbors dozing in recliners connected to oxygen concentrators powered by her generator.

Then Sam checked on her guests. Mrs. Fitzpatrick and Mr. Daniels were settled comfortably in the living room with their oxygen concentrators humming quietly. The house seemed oddly quiet after the bustle of activity throughout the day.

Sam noticed a note on the kitchen counter, written in Nora's precise handwriting:

Sam,

Franklin's mother came by. She finished her hospital shift early and picked him up at 7:30. I've gone home as my roof is intact, unlike half the neighborhood (shoddy construction, if you ask me). Mrs. Peterson will arrive at 8 AM for her insulin. I've left Precious's tutu here – he refuses to wear it during "disaster relief operations" as it "undermines his authority." We'll be at the clubhouse at 7 AM sharp tomorrow to continue organizing the neighborhood response.

– Nora

P.S. Your emergency kit is woefully lacking in hard candies. I've made a list of suggested improvements on the back of this note.

P.P.S. Go to sleep!

Sam smiled at the note's unmistakable Nora-ness. She flipped it over to find, sure enough, a detailed list of "critical items" her emergency supplies were missing, including butterscotch candies, proper tea (not those "silly tea bags"), and matching emergency blankets "for aesthetic purposes during crises."

After a quick bowl of soup, Sam made sure the generator was still running smoothly. She added oil to be safe. Then she made a final call on the walkie-talkie to the clubhouse to check in on Aiden.

"Everything's quiet here," he said, his voice slightly distorted by the static. "Get some rest. Tomorrow's going to be another long day."

"Still planning to check on Victor Reid at the old library tomorrow morning?" asked Sam.

"I'll meet you there at nine."

After a quick shower that felt like heaven after the day's grime, Sam collapsed into bed with Arlo curled against her side. The little dog seemed to sense her exhaustion, staying closer than usual. Despite her tiredness, sleep didn't immediately come. Her mind kept circling back to Harrison Blackwood's body, the unnatural arrangement of the debris, and the strange marks on his clothing.

Sam turned onto her side, and Arlo adjusted himself against the curve of her knees. The familiar warmth of his small body finally helped her racing thoughts slow down.

Chapter Seven

Morning came a little too quickly, with golden sunlight streaming through the gaps in the curtains. Sam blinked awake, momentarily disoriented until the events of the previous day came rushing back.

Arlo was already awake, watching her with his soulful eyes. He wagged his tail when she looked at him.

"Good morning to you too," Sam said, her voice rough with sleep. She glanced at her watch, seeing it was 7:15. She had time to check on the guests, make breakfast, and still meet Aiden at the old library by nine.

Sam quickly showered and dressed, then headed to the kitchen. She'd told her senior guests to make themselves at home, but wasn't completely convinced they were going to do so. She decided to make omelets and keep them warm in her slow cooker. They might be a little dried out, but she decided her guests might be willing to make the sacrifice for a warm breakfast that was ready-made.

Then she gave Arlo an abbreviated walk to the front entrance and back. She put a pair of dog socks on him first, just in case there were splinters of wood from the debris that might catch in his paws. After she got back home, she gave Arlo a couple of treats, then took off for the old library.

Sam was later glad she left the house when she did. The debris in the roads made the drive slow-going. When she finally made it to the old library, she saw Aiden's car already there.

The former library was a gorgeous old building, and Sam could see why a preservationist like Victor would have wanted to save it from demolition. It was no longer being used because the town of Sunset Ridge had outgrown it and had constructed a new building to better suit its needs. It was a rambling three-story Victorian structure built in 1895. The tall arched windows that lined its façade were now boarded up. Sam was glad to see the storm hadn't damaged the building too badly, although there were trees down on the property, one leaning precariously on the side of the library.

Aiden gave her a wave and walked over. "How are things at your place?"

"Everything seems pretty good. The generator is running with no issues, although I feel like I should be knocking on wood. I wonder when the power lines will start being repaired."

Aiden shook his head. "It's going to be a while. From what I heard on the radio this morning, the roads are still blocked for any linemen to get in. After we talk to Victor, I was planning on taking my chainsaw out and helping do some clearing. If we wait for the county to handle it, it's going to take forever."

The door to the old library was locked, so Aiden banged loudly on it. He gave Sam a rueful look. "Unfortunately, the area where Victor is living is on the third floor. It might take him a minute."

It did, in fact, take a few minutes before a rumpled-looking Victor opened the door. He was a tall a lanky man with prematurely graying dark hair. To complete the ex-professor look, he wore a pair of wire-rimmed glasses. He seemed to have coffee stains on his shirt. "Aiden," he said absently. "Everything okay?" He gave Sam a bemused smile.

Aiden introduced Sam to Victor, and he gave her a little bow, which she thought he meant to be facetious, but then appeared to be completely genuine. She wasn't sure what to do in response, so she just gave him a smile.

Then Victor narrowed his eyes. "Wait, I know who you are. You live in that historic home in Maple Hills, right?"

"The very one."

Victor said, "And you're *not* selling the property to Harrison Blackwood."

"No," said Sam. "I had no intention of doing that. And now, of course, it would be impossible."

Victor tilted his head quizzically to one side. Aiden said, "Harrison is dead, Victor."

Sam was sure she spotted a look of relief pass over Victor's features before he said, "You're kidding me. Don't tell me, let me guess. Heart attack. That guy was always so intense."

Sam thought Victor could win some intensity contests, himself.

Aiden said, "No, it seems to be a storm-related death." He glanced quickly over at Sam, and she gave an almost imperceptible nod of her head to indicate she'd definitely go along with not mentioning the suspicious circumstances around Harrison's death.

"Weird for him to be traipsing around in a storm like that," said Victor. "But then I always thought he was odd. I mean, it seemed like greed was his sole motivator. How can you not appreciate the beauty of an old building like this?"

Sam cleared her throat. "Actually, I haven't been inside the old library. It was closed to the public by the time I moved to Sunset Ridge."

Victor blinked at her. "Heavens, I didn't even invite you two in. My poor mother must be rolling in her grave. Come in and see my makeshift home."

The inside of the building was dark, and it took a few moments for Sam's eyes to adjust. When they did, she said, "Oh, it's beautiful."

This obviously pleased Victor. "Isn't it? I'm so glad you can see beyond the dust and neglect. The bones of this old lady are lovely. This was the grand reading room." He eagerly waved them further inside.

The room had ceilings that must have been sixteen feet high. The original oak bookshelves still lined the walls, though they'd long been emptied of books. The ornate plaster ceiling medallions were cracking in places. The most striking feature was a glass floor mezzanine that would have allowed natural light from the tall windows if they hadn't been boarded up.

"Want to see my personal space?" asked Victor.

"Oh, I wouldn't want to intrude," said Sam.

"Nonsense. I'd like to show it to you." Victor fidgeted with his sleeve. "Sadly, I've recently lost my university job, so I've temporarily relocated here. The town was happy to allow me to stay since I was helping to protect the building from development while they figure out their next steps."

They walked upstairs to what had been a reading nook. Architectural drawings were pinned haphazardly on the walls and his desk was buried under papers, blueprints, and coffee cups. There was evidence of takeout meals and microwave dinners. A box labeled "University Office", presumably holding the contents of his desk at the university, was still taped up and seemingly unpacked.

"Excuse the mess," said Victor apologetically. He ran his hands through his already-disheveled hair as he took in the room. He made a half-hearted attempt to throw some wrappers into a trash bag sitting on the floor.

Sam noticed Victor quickly cover up some papers. She caught a glimpse of handwritten calculations, printed odds sheets, and what looked like pre-paid credit cards.

"Here," said Victor, pulling out a blueprint. "Here's an old blueprint of your home, Sam. I don't know if you got something like this at your closing."

Sam took the paper from him. "No, I sure didn't. Do you mind if I take a photo of it?"

"Not at all." While Sam was doing that, Victor pulled out a couple of metal folding chairs. He brushed the dust off so Sam and Aiden could sit before settling into a camping-style chair.

Aiden said, "I just wanted to check on you after the storm."

Victor gave him a tight smile. "Thanks. I'm doing okay, but it was a loud, long night. I didn't get any sleep, but I caught up a little last night." Despite his words, he had an exhausted air about him. "How did everything go with the two of you?"

Aiden shook his head. "Just some debris in the yard. It could have been a lot worse."

Sam said, "Same, really. There are a couple of trees down on the property, but nothing hit the house."

"Well, now, that *is* a relief," said Victor, pushing his glasses up his nose. "That house has stood proudly since the mid-to-late 1800s. I'd hate to think a random storm could take it out."

"The random storm was a pretty big deal," said Aiden slowly. "Have you been outside at all since it happened?"

Victor shook his head wearily. "No. I've been working on looking at old blueprints. And sleeping. Obviously, no power and no internet, so I have no idea what the big picture is here. All I know is that I had to have cold coffee yesterday and today. Was there a lot of damage? How long before they get everything back up and running?"

Sam said, "It's going to be a while. From the little I've seen and heard, crews are going to have a tough time getting into town because the roads are blocked with debris."

Victor said, "Got it. Sorry to hear that. Any loss of life, or have you heard?"

Sam said slowly, "Just Harrison Blackwood."

"Ah, right. How quickly I forget. You'd just told me that. Although, I must say that if somebody had to die during the storm, I can't think of a better candidate."

"Did you know him well?" asked Sam.

"The guy was frankly a huge thorn in my side. He would have tackled any structure in town for development, it didn't matter whether it was historical or not. Harrison had absolutely no respect for architecture or anything else." Victor's voice had developed an edge. "He was a waste of space."

Sam wasn't surprised to hear it, but was surprised by Victor's vehemence. She would have liked to have heard a little more about Victor's perspective on Harrison, but he switched topics, looking back over at Aiden. "So not much damage to your place. Everything else going okay?" he asked.

"Yeah, it's all right. The storm clean-up is kind of priority number one right now, I guess."

Victor frowned. "Really? Not teaching?"

"Well, I'm not going to be able to do much teaching without power. And water is probably going to be the next thing that's threatened, depending on how the supply has been impacted. School's going to likely be out for weeks."

Victor looked thoughtfully out the window at the toppled trees outside. "I see. I guess I should spend more time outside. I have the habit of getting buried with research and various projects."

Aiden gave him a concerned look. "Any leads on the job hunt?"

Victor sighed. "No, I'm afraid not. But it hasn't been my priority. It's a funny thing. Doing historical preservation work was always something I did on the side. Teaching was what usually brought in the income."

"You're not looking to transfer to another university somewhere else?" asked Sam.

Victor shook his head. "No, that would drive me crazy to have to uproot myself and move somewhere else. If something opens up that I can commute to, that would be a different story."

But Sam knew the colleges nearby were small ones that probably didn't have the room or budget for bringing in more staff.

Aiden must have thought the same thing because he winced a little. "Okay, man. Well, you have to follow your gut."

"It's more like I'm following my heart," said Victor with a shrug. "If money was the most important thing to me, I'd end up just like Harrison Blackwood. Greed can't be the primary motivator."

Aiden said, "Unlike Harrison."

"Yeah." Victor suddenly looked sharply at Aiden. "Do you know something I don't?"

"What do you mean?"

Victor said, "I know how close you are to the cops you once worked with. Was Harrison's death storm-related? Or was it something else?"

Although Victor seemed to mostly be an absent-minded professor, he apparently still could be intuitive and shrewd. He seemed to have zeroed in on the crux of the matter when it came to Harrison's untimely demise.

"That's something they'll have to conclude," said Aiden. "But it's a possibility, sure."

Victor grunted. "That makes sense." He quickly said, "I didn't like him, obviously. But I didn't rush him to meet his maker, either. I was right here in the building whenever it was that he died."

Aiden gave him a wry smile. "When an actual active police officer asks you for an alibi, they're probably going to want you to narrow it down a little better than that."

"It'll be the same answer, no matter what time or day they ask me about. I've been in the building for days now."

Sam thought again about the notebook she'd glimpsed with the handwritten calculations, the odds sheets, and the pre-paid credit cards. It could have somehow had something to do with historic preservation, but it still struck her as odd.

"Can you think of anybody who might want Harrison dead?" asked Aiden.

Victor snorted inelegantly. "Everybody."

"More specifically?"

Victor said, "Well, one person who comes to mind is Trevor Mills."

Sam was sorry to hear Trevor's name come up again. When Charlotte had mentioned him at the bookstore, she'd hoped it was just Charlotte's opinion.

Victor continued, pushing his glasses up his nose. "Harrison threatened his livelihood. Trevor's company specializes in historic restoration with techniques that have been in his family for generations. Harrison awarded a massive renovation contract for the hotel's east wing to an out-of-state company that uses cheaper, modern materials."

"But wouldn't that be Harrison's right as the property owner?" Aiden asked, leaning forward slightly.

Victor gave a short laugh. "Sure, if that's all it was. But Trevor told me Harrison blackballed him with other developers after Trevor pointed out code violations in the plans. Harrison called him 'outdated' and 'difficult to work with' to anyone who would listen."

Sam thought about the careful work she'd seen Trevor do around Maple Hills. "That would certainly hurt his reputation."

"Worse than that," Victor said, his voice lowering. "Trevor had invested heavily in specialized equipment for the hotel project. For equipment he's still paying for. And his daughter Angie's college fund was tied up in it too. I heard Trevor confronted Harrison at the town council meeting last month. He said Harrison's chosen contractor was using substandard materials that wouldn't hold up in mountain weather."

"Was he right?" Sam asked.

"We'll never know now," Victor said, his expression darkening again momentarily. "But I think Trevor was probably right."

Then Victor abruptly changed the subject, chatting garrulously instead about the old library and his goals for saving it.

"Well, we'll get out of your hair, Victor," Aiden said, standing after a few minutes. "I just wanted to check in. You have enough food and everything?"

Victor looked surprised, as if he'd forgotten about food. "I do, but most of it's in the fridge."

"Is it food that has to be cooked?" asked Sam.

"Good question." Victor looked thoughtful. "Most of it needs a microwave, yeah. I'm a fan of microwave meals. But I have some cheese in there I could eat. I guess I should keep the fridge closed unless I absolutely need to open it. Or I can go to the store to pick up food that doesn't need refrigeration."

"Might want to do that now," said Aiden. "From what I hear, the stores are already selling out of that kind of stuff. And, since there's no internet for them to receive debit or credit cards, you have to pay in cash."

Now Victor looked even more surprised. "Cash only? I never have cash on me. What about ATMs?"

"There aren't any that work because the power is still out everywhere."

Victor made a face. "Maybe the linemen will get the power up soon. Crews will probably make the main roads a priority."

Aiden said, "I wouldn't count on it, man. I'd lend you some, but I don't have a lot of cash, myself."

"I don't really use cash, either," said Sam. However, she did have a small safe with cash in it, just to be on the safe side. But she'd rather reserve that either for herself or for folks in her neighborhood in a similar situation as Victor.

"No worries. I'll stretch out what I've got in the meantime," said Victor with a shrug. "Thanks for coming by, guys."

Chapter Eight

A couple of minutes later, Aiden and Sam were standing by their cars. Aiden gave Sam a rueful look. "I get the feeling Victor wasn't quite as prepared for the hurricane as you were."

"Hopefully he'll get by all right, though." Sam paused. "Did you see what I saw on Victor's desk?"

"A lot of boring blueprints and architectural stuff?" asked Aiden dryly. "Along with maybe some cracker crumbs?"

"Well, that for sure. But I couldn't help but notice some things that made me wonder if Victor might be gambling."

"Uh-oh." Aiden frowned.

"I don't know a lot about it, but there were sports betting odds sheets that had been printed out. He'd circled some stuff and had made calculations in the margins. And there were betting site names in an account balance ledger he had lying there. DraftKings and PokerStars and things like that were in it."

Aiden grimaced. "I hate to hear that. Victor had a gambling problem a few years ago, but managed to quit. Maybe it's the reason he lost his job. When he's gambling, it's like this all-encompassing thing. It could have meant he was slacking at work."

Sam said, "Maybe he was just cleaning up and getting rid of some of that stuff."

"I'd like to think that's the case, but his manner made me think something was wrong, too. Victor just seemed off." He paused. "What did you make of what he was saying about Trevor?"

"I hope Trevor had nothing to do with Harrison's death because I really like the guy. He's helped me out with the house on a few occasions, and I thought he was not only super-professional, but a terrific person. Plus, his daughter, Angie, is awesome, too."

Aiden said, "I taught her a couple of years ago. She's what now . . . a senior?"

"That's right. A senior. Angie's helped me walk Arlo when Franklin wasn't available and I've gone out of town. She's a great girl. She's trying to get volunteer hours, like your students, and checked in with Nora at the house when I was out yesterday. Nora asked her to help out at the clubhouse today. As far as I know, she's over there now."

Aiden raised his eyebrow. "That's especially generous, considering she doesn't live in the neighborhood."

"True. But Trevor and Angie aren't far away, either. Do you think Trevor's the kind of guy who'd get that bent out of shape over a work issue? Mad enough to kill someone, I mean?"

Aiden said, "I don't really know him all that well. Luckily, any work I've needed for the house has been stuff I can handle, myself. But when I was a detective, I was always amazed how people could lash out and commit murder. Unpremeditated, of course, but just as deadly."

"I hope he's not involved." She paused. "Are you heading back home or going back out to help?"

"I think I'll go see if I can lend a hand with clearing the other entrance to the neighborhood. There were a couple of other guys with chainsaws who are planning on meeting up with me to see if we can open it back up."

A bit later, Sam pulled into her driveway. She wanted to head to the clubhouse to see how everything was there, but thought she should check on her guests first. Sam figured walking Arlo over to the clubhouse might be a good idea, too. The little guy could use some exercise, and maybe he could act as something of a support animal over there. It had been a stressful last twenty-four hours for everybody.

When she went inside her house, she saw immediately that Nora and Precious were back. Nora appeared to be playing cards with the other seniors. A large bowl of popcorn was on the table and the fixed expressions on Arlo and Precious's faces indicated that there had perhaps been some spillage, accidental or not, from the bowl.

Her guests appeared to have crafted makeshift poker chips out of Sam's emergency food stash. Nora gave her a smug look when she saw Sam was peering at the odd display on the table. "Travel size cereal boxes are low stakes, granola bars are medium stakes, and the chocolate bars are high stakes."

Sam fervently hoped they wouldn't be eating the chips at the end of the game. At least not the chocolate, since it appeared it was going to be difficult to replace them with the grocery stores in their current condition.

She felt afraid to ask the next question. "And the jackpot?"

"Beef jerky strips."

That was fine with Sam.

Mrs. Fitzpatrick chimed in, "There's a house rule that oxygen tank users get an extra card."

Nora suddenly looked cranky. "Even though the oxygen tank users seem to be much better at poker."

"We don't have Franklin today?" asked Sam, glancing around.

Nora looked even crankier. "His mom is at home sleeping after the long shift at the hospital. But maybe she'll be called in later."

"We rearranged your pantry," chirped another senior.

Nora smirked at the panic on Sam's face. One of Sam's resolutions had been to be more flexible with things that didn't really matter much. The pantry should fall under that category. However, she did have her pantry configured in a very particular manner. "How so?" asked Sam, trying to make the question sound casual.

Mrs. Fitzpatrick said, "We created an A.U.R. system. That's an apocalypse usefulness rating."

"Although there has been some spirited debate over what qualifies," said Nora.

Mrs. Fitzpatrick said, "Each item gets five stars for immediate survival value."

"What might qualify for that?" asked Sam. "Canned meats?"

"Indeed!" said the old woman. "Tuna, especially."

"Only because you like tuna so much," said Nora with a disdainful sniff. "I think beans are better, personally."

"Do I even *have* items that are low on the scale?" Sam prided herself with her healthful eating. But she had to wonder.

"Yes, we had a few one-star items that we labeled as empty calories," said Mrs. Fitzpatrick. "Rice cakes, for one."

Sam frowned. "Rice cakes aren't terrible for you."

"What about the marshmallows?" asked Nora, tilting her head to one side.

Precious and Arlo also tilted their heads, as if they understood exactly what she was referring to.

"Oh, those are for hot chocolate," said Sam.

Nora said, "If you say so. Mr. Daniels here also came up with a category. Would you like to explain it?" she asked the old man.

He cleared his throat. "Morale essentials. Because we have to keep our spirits up, you see."

"A smart idea," said Sam. "What qualifies for that category?"

"Coffee, chocolate, and cookies," Mr. Daniels answered promptly.

Further digging on the pantry system was interrupted when Sam's friend, Olivia, walked in. Her cheeks were flushed from exertion—likely from trudging up Sam's steep driveway. Sam walked away from the poker playing seniors to speak with her.

"How's everything going with the food distribution for the pantry?" she asked.

Olivia smiled at her. "It's going better than I thought. Jason has helped me take some food to a few shut-ins in other neighborhoods late yesterday. The roads haven't really opened up as quickly as I'd like, so we've had to park the car and just hike in to some streets. But the folks were so glad to get it."

Sam smiled back at her. Olivia had gone through some tough times lately and a health crisis in the not-too-distant past. It was good to see her confident and feeling rewarded by volunteering.

"Have you happened to see Trevor Mills when you've been out with Jason?" asked Sam.

"Sure, he's been working like crazy, from what I've seen. He was clearing debris downtown just a few minutes ago." Olivia glanced at her watch. "I'd better grab the cold food and head on out again. Jason and I want to make a few more deliveries. Thanks again for letting us keep some food here at your place. We're trying to come up with a better solution soon. The community center is trying to pull something together, like you suggested."

Sam said, "It's my pleasure. I just wish the power would come back on for the rest of you. And speaking of my generator, I better check and make sure it has plenty of oil."

But when she went outside, she found it was low. She quickly topped it off, then headed out to the clubhouse with Arlo to see how things were going there.

On the way over, she saw neighborhood debris piled on the curbs—a good sign things were starting to get back to normal. Neighbors were helping other neighbors with minor repairs. And Alfred's hand-painted signs directed residents to the clubhouse for resources.

A portable generator was humming efficiently outside the clubhouse, and a blue tarp covered the section of the roof that was damaged. She greeted neighbors who were standing in line for the charging station set up on the clubhouse porch, under the awning. Sam was pleased to see the bulletin board inside was covered with neighborhood needs and offers. Then she saw Angie, Trevor's daughter, who was in the process of sorting supplies into three sections of a long table: medical supplies, food distribution, and tool lending.

"Oh my gosh, Arlo!" Angie said, coming over to give him a cuddle. Arlo wagged his tail and looked lovingly into her face. "I've missed you, buddy." She looked up at Sam. "Sorry I've been AWOL lately. I had tons of tests at school, so I was stuck inside studying all the time. I missed walking him."

"Don't even think about it. School always comes first," said Sam firmly. "I've been walking him a good deal myself, and we've had lots of days with the agility group, too." She glanced around. "How are things here?"

"I think we're pretty much set up," said Angie, looking around the room with satisfaction. "The tools are coming and going back out again pretty regularly with people borrowing them. Especially the chainsaws."

Sam winced. "Hopefully everybody is being careful with those. The last thing anybody needs is a medical emergency right now."

"True."

Sam glanced over to a small table and chair at the back of the room. An expensive-looking camera sat on top. "What's that over there?"

Angie smiled. "I've been taking photos of the damage—some of it for my high school paper and some of it for my dad for insurance claim stuff."

"Did your house get damaged during the storm?"

"Yeah," said Angie. "Nothing too bad, but there was damage to the garage when a tree hit that part of the house." She walked over to the table and grabbed the camera to show Sam some of the digital pictures she'd taken.

Sam could tell she had a real eye for photography. Not only that, when Angie was describing the damage in the photos, she used precise architectural terminology.

"You seem to know a lot about... well, actually, a good deal. Architecture and photography both, for sure," said Sam. "Are those things you're looking to study in college?"

Angie smiled. "Oh, I'm just dabbling in it. I don't really know what I want to major in. I have lots of interests." Arlo nuzzled her leg, and she stooped down. "Like Arlo. I could totally see myself as a vet. But yeah, I think I've picked up a lot from my dad. Not the photography, but anything that overlaps with contracting. Yesterday, I was helping him out as much as I could because he was swamped with emergency repairs. Of course he still is, but I needed a break from it for a little while today."

Sam chuckled. "I'm not sure organizing supplies at our clubhouse qualifies as a break, but I really appreciate it."

"Oh, I liked the opportunity to help out. When the storm came through, it felt like everything was outside our control, you know? It's kind of a way of regaining that control."

Sam said, "Believe me, I totally understand that."

Angie's phone chimed, and she pulled it out of her pocket. "Actually, looks like Dad is going to swing by and pick me up. He needs me to help out at this site he's going to be at today."

Sam had been hoping to find a time she could casually talk to Trevor without it being too obvious she was trying to find out more about Harrison's death. But it didn't sound like this was going to be the best time to do it unless she could stall him for a while. "Hey, why don't the two of you grab a bite to eat from the fridge here? As a thank you for your helping out at the clubhouse. We have a lot of food here."

"You don't have to do that. I was happy to help out."

Sam said, "I know, but still. Plus, I haven't actually eaten myself since really early."

"Sure, that sounds good. I'll ask Dad when he comes in. I'm not sure if he has to be at the site he's heading to right away, or if he has some leeway."

Chapter Nine

Trevor arrived a few minutes later. He was in his mid-forties with a muscular build and calloused hands from his work. He was wearing his usual flannel shirt and well-worn jeans. Arlo greeted him happily, and he stooped to pet the little dog, who immediately flopped on the floor for a belly rub.

As it happened, Trevor hadn't eaten a bite the entire day. Angie shook her head. "You can't do that, Dad. You won't be fueled up for work if you don't pace yourself and make sure you eat and hydrate."

Trevor said lightly, "Yes, Mom." He turned to Sam. "Angie has apparently made it a personal mission to take care of me."

"Somebody has to," said Angie. Her phone made an alert again, and she said, "I'll just grab a sandwich and make a phone call. Sharon was going to update me on a friend of ours who basically lost her house in a mudslide." She grabbed one of the premade ham and cheese sandwiches from the fridge and headed for the community room to lounge on the sofa there.

Trevor and Sam settled into the chairs at the table in the clubhouse kitchen.

"From what Angie was telling me, it sounds like you had some damage to your house."

Trevor sighed, his shoulders sagging slightly. "Yeah. A tree took out part of the garage roof." He ran a hand through his hair, leaving it standing slightly on end. "Nothing I can't handle with repairs, though, thankfully. But I've got to wait until an insurance adjuster makes it out until I take care of it. Otherwise, it's out of my pocket."

"That's frustrating," Sam said, noticing the dark circles under his eyes. "Waiting must be hard when you know how to fix it yourself."

"Exactly." Trevor's expression softened. "Angie's been a big help, though. She actually has been managing the insurance stuff, took pictures, documented everything. That girl's got a head for details."

"She's going to be a standout at college next year," said Sam. "She's so driven." They could hear Angie talking on the phone to her friend in the next room, her voice bubbly.

A smile broke through Trevor's exhaustion. "She sure is." He leaned forward, lowering his voice. "And I appreciate the help you gave her with those college applications and essay reviews. I tried, but you know." He shook his head. "I'm better with hammer and nails than commas and semicolons."

"Happy to help," Sam said. "She made it easy because her writing was already strong."

They chatted for a couple more minutes about the storm damage and recovery efforts. Then Sam broached the subject of Harrison's death.

"I heard about Harrison Blackwood," Sam said carefully, watching his reaction. "Were the two of you acquainted?"

Trevor's fingers tightened around his cup. "Harrison?" His voice hardened noticeably. "Yeah, I know him." He blinked, then looked at her more sharply. "Wait, what about him? What are you saying?"

"He died during the storm," Sam said, noting how Trevor's posture changed. "I thought you might have heard."

Trevor stared at her, genuine shock crossing his features. "Dead? Harrison is dead?" He sat back in his chair, processing. "I just saw him a few days ago, before the storm hit."

"I'm sorry to be the one to tell you," Sam said. "The news hasn't spread the way it usually does with the phones and internet down."

Trevor ran a hand across his beard. "That's just, wow." He shook his head slowly. "I can't believe it. How did it happen?"

"He was found outside after the storm," Sam said, intentionally keeping the details vague. "Were you two friends?"

"Friends?" Trevor gave a short, humorless laugh that didn't reach his eyes. "No, not even close. We butted heads constantly." He stared down at his coffee, then back at Sam. "But dead? I never would've wished that on him."

"It sounds like there was some history there," Sam observed.

Trevor's jaw tightened. "Harrison could be difficult. No, not just difficult . . . destructive. To the town and its history." He took a deep breath. "You know those beautiful cornices on the Ridgeview House hotel? My grandfather installed those in 1952. My father maintained them in the '80s. I did the restoration work five years ago."

charged me a dime for the lessons." He shook his head. "It kills me to think of them using that money. Fifteen years of saving, and it was finally about to do some good."

Sam's mind was already whirring with possibilities. "Let me reach out to some people. Although that's harder to do with the cell tower down. Maybe there's something we can come up with so they won't have to dip into that fund." She made a mental note to start organizing this effort as soon as possible.

Angie joined them with a smile, interrupting Sam's planning. "I think lunch was the right call. I feel so much better now."

Trevor's demeanor instantly brightened at the sight of his daughter. "I do, too. But I hate to admit it when you're right."

Arlo bounded back over to Angie, and she picked him up to cuddle him. "I'll come by soon to walk this little guy again, okay, Sam? I could use exercise, too. I feel like most of what I've been doing lately is sitting and studying."

Trevor stood, giving a stretch before tossing his plate and Angie's in the trash. "Well, you'll have the opportunity to get some exercise in right now, Ang, helping me out at the Jones site." He gave her a grin.

She shook her head with a laugh. "Got it. Sounds like a fun afternoon, Dad. See you later, Sam."

Sam finished doing the sorting that Angie had nearly finished. Then the door to the clubhouse opened and a woman peered in. Ginny Wilson, her friend from agility, grinned when she spotted Sam. "There you are! I've been looking for you. The lady at your house told me you were down here." She reached down to rub Arlo vigorously, which Arlo apparently loved.

"That was probably Nora. What's up, Ginny? Is everything going okay?"

Ginny said, "Hmm? Oh, you mean because I was hunting you down? Yeah, it's all good. Well, sort of. We've all got lots of stress and no cell service, power, or internet, but it could be a lot worse, couldn't it? Anyway, I was thinking we should all have an emergency mental health break. It would be good for the pups too, wouldn't it? After all, I've read all this stuff about dogs absorbing their humans' stress and I totally believe it. How about if we have an impromptu mixer? I've rounded up most of the gang."

"Sure, that sounds good. Over at the agility course?"

Ginny shook her head. "The field is damaged and is going to need clearing. It's going to be a while. But I figured we all needed to clear our own properties first, before we worried about the agility course. I thought we'd meet at my house. We won't be doing agility, but I've got a big, fenced-in yard for the pups to play in and we can all visit and commiserate with each other. You up for it?"

"Count me in. When?"

Ginny looked at her watch and chuckled. "Right now. It took me longer to find you than I planned on. Everybody's probably over there now. Scoop up Arlo and come along."

Sam did. At first, part of her thought she should run back to the house first. That she should check in on the folks who were staying there. But then she realized Ginny was right. Sam felt stressed out. In fact, her jaw was set so tightly that it was starting to hurt. A little time away would be good for her and Arlo, too. And it was, finally, a beautiful day.

Ginny's yard ended up being a great spot for an impromptu gathering. She had a bunch of old bowls set out for the dogs to drink water. The yard was partly in the sun and partly in the shade of a massive oak tree. She had lots of mismatched old yard chairs for folks to sit in. Sam was impressed at the number of agility club members Ginny had been able to round up, especially considering the fact that she'd had to go by in person to find them.

And she saw with interest that Diane Foster was there with her corgi, Echo. Echo was grinning a tremendous corgi grin, looking positively delighted to be out and about with other dogs. Diane looked tired, but was tracking Echo as she happily chased a golden retriever around the yard. Sam hoped she could casually introduce the subject of Harrison and get the details about Diane's interactions with him. It sounded like she'd had some conflicts with him over environmental issues.

Chapter Ten

But speaking with Diane wasn't immediately to be. Ginny, who was quite the talker, had plopped down next to Diane for a chat. Whatever Ginny was talking about, she was quite animated as she discussed it, waving her hands around. So instead, Sam joined them and watched as Arlo joyfully made circuits around the yard, tongue lolling out of his mouth as he ran.

As Sam expected, Ginny pulled her right into the conversation. They made small talk for a while, laughing at the dogs who were acting like children in their excitement to be outside and have a bit of normalcy.

Then Ginny got distracted by another conversation and jumped up to join it, leaving Diane and Sam by themselves. Diane was a tall and athletic woman in her mid-thirties with her dark hair in a braid. "Glad you came, Sam. I didn't make it the last couple of weeks because life got busy. Then I realized how much Echo and I missed seeing all of you."

"We missed you, too," said Sam. "Have things settled down now? Hurricanes aside?"

Diane laughed. "Yeah, the hurricane was a rude awakening, wasn't it? I have a couple of trees down. Unfortunately, one of them is on the house. But Echo and I are safe, so that's all that really matters, isn't it? I don't know if things at work have actually settled down or not, because I haven't been able to follow up on anything with the cell service and internet being down. Maybe that's a blessing in disguise."

"Remind me again what work you do? I know it's environmental in nature."

Diane watched as Echo and Arlo started playing chase in the fenced yard. "I used to be an environmental lawyer in D.C. But I got burned out and decided to move down here to do environmental activism. My dad lives down here, too. You might know him; he owns the nature center in town."

"Oh, he must love that you're local again. And I'm guessing that you like the slower pace here in Sunset Ridge."

"It's great to be with Dad. But I'm starting to wonder if my burnout is actually something to do with me instead of what I'm doing," she said wryly. "I've gotten just as burned out dealing with environmental issues here as I did in a courtroom in Washington."

"I'm sorry to hear that. What kinds of issues are you running into?"

Diane sighed. "The issues, as usual, are with humans, not with whatever other species I'm involved with. Take, for instance, the rare bat species I've been focused on lately."

"I think I read about the bats in the paper," said Sam. "Although I can't remember all the details."

Diane looked pleased that Sam was familiar with it. "Basically, the historic hotel downtown has rare bats living in its attic. The hotel had no idea, of course. I found out about it via the wildlife removal team they'd contacted because they heard noises up there and thought it might be mice. Anyway, it was quite a find."

"I'm guessing the hotel wasn't happy about preserving them?"

Diane shook her head. "No. There's a local developer who'd purchased the hotel and was planning on renovating it. Naturally, his planned approach was to totally modernize the place with no care for its historic or environmental attributes. He was furious with me for bringing the bats to his attention."

"That would be Harrison Blackwood?" Sam asked, watching as Arlo and Echo tumbled playfully across the grass.

Diane nodded. "You know him?"

"Knew," Sam corrected gently. "He was found at the hotel during the storm. He didn't make it."

Diane's hand froze halfway to her water bottle. "You're kidding me." She looked genuinely shocked. "Harrison is dead? How did it happen?"

"The initial assessment is storm-related," Sam said, carefully keeping her voice neutral. "He was outside during the worst of it."

Diane shook her head slowly. "I can't believe it. That doesn't sound like Harrison at all. He was the type to hunker down in luxury while everyone else dealt with a crisis." She frowned. "I'm sorry. That wasn't very charitable of me."

"You had issues with him over the bats?" Sam prompted, keeping her tone conversational.

"Issues is putting it mildly." Diane tucked a loose strand of hair back into her braid. "When I monitored the colonies in the hotel attic, I filed for emergency protected status. Harrison tried to cover up a negative environmental impact study that would have stopped his renovation plans."

Echo bounded over, tongue lolling and eyes bright with excitement. The corgi flopped onto Diane's feet, panting happily. Diane automatically reached down to scratch behind his ears. Echo closed his eyes in bliss.

"That sounds serious," Sam said.

"It was. The species is on the brink of extinction, and the hotel attic and the finials on the roof provide one of their last viable habitats." Diane's voice grew passionate. "Harrison claimed the documentation was fabricated. He even tried to access the attic at night to 'verify' the colonies weren't there." Her fingers made air quotes.

"What was he planning to do with the hotel?" Sam asked. "You mentioned modernizing it. Are the renovations supposed to be extensive?"

"Harrison wanted to gut it. Replace all the historic features with modern amenities." Diane's lips pressed together in a thin line. "But that's just the way he was. He just did what he wanted and expected everyone to step out of his way. My father's nature center would have lost its parking access too, since Harrison owned that lot as well."

"That would have been devastating for the center."

"Devastating for my father, too. That place is his life's work." Diane's eyes followed Echo as the dog rejoined the playful group. "I confronted Harrison at the town meeting last month about it. It got a little heated."

Sam nodded encouragingly. "I can imagine. Considering you were dealing with something that's important to you."

Diane looked away, her eyes tracking the dogs playing. "I told him I would do whatever it took to protect those bats." She turned back to Sam, her expression troubled. "But I'm not happy he's gone. His death is a real tragedy."

"No, of course you're not happy about it," Sam said quickly. "Is the habitat still secure now?"

"For the moment. But who knows what happens to his properties now?" Diane's brow furrowed. "I was actually planning to assess the colonies again after the storm to ensure they weren't affected."

"You have access to the hotel attic?" Sam asked.

"I have a special permit for environmental monitoring." Diane pulled a lanyard from her pocket with an official-looking badge. "It gives me access to protected habitats, even on private property."

Sam watched as Arlo attempted to herd a much larger golden retriever, his small body buzzing with determination. "Had you been up there recently? Before the storm?"

Diane hesitated. "Actually, yes. Shortly before the storm. I was checking on them because changes in barometric pressure can affect their behavior." She smiled as Echo darted between the retriever's legs. "Harrison seemed to already be working on the hotel, which irritated me. There was scaffolding on the east side of the building."

"That's where Harrison was found."

Diane looked at her curiously. "You were there?"

"I helped discover him," Sam admitted. "I was with Kevin Zhang shortly after he heard Harrison was missing."

"Kevin Zhang," Diane repeated thoughtfully. "Harrison's former business partner. They had quite the falling out, from what I heard."

"Making enemies seemed to be something of a habit for Harrison."

Diane gave a short laugh. "You could say that. Between the environmental groups, the historical preservation society, and the local businesses he was pressuring, Harrison wasn't winning any popularity contests."

They watched as Arlo attempted an ambitious leap over a much taller dog and landed with surprising grace. "It's hard to imagine all those projects just coming to a total halt now."

Diane took a sip from her water bottle. "I doubt they'll stop. Someone will step in. That's the nature of development; it finds a way." She gave a wry smile.

"Was anyone else was particularly at odds with him?" Sam kept her tone casual. "Besides you and the environmental groups, I mean. And Kevin."

"Besides half the town?" Diane laughed, but there was little humor in it. "Charlotte Webb was fighting him tooth and nail over her bookstore. Did you know the building has been in her family for three generations?"

Sam shook her head.

"It's more than just a business to her," said Diane. "When Harrison tried to buy her out, Charlotte actually took out additional loans to improve the property and make it harder for him to claim it was blighted."

"What do you mean by claiming it was blighted?"

"Oh, it's a developer's tactic," Diane explained, her environmental lawyer background showing. "If a property falls into disrepair, developers can sometimes get the town to declare it 'blighted'—essentially a hazard or eyesore. Then they can push for redevelopment under public interest claims, sometimes even forcing a sale. Charlotte wasn't going to give Harrison that opportunity."

Sam nodded thoughtfully. "So she took on debt to make improvements and protect her building."

"Exactly. Harrison wasn't expecting that level of resistance." Diane shook her head. "I've never seen someone so calm in the face of threats. But Charlotte can be fierce when it comes to that bookstore." Diane lowered her voice slightly. "I saw them arguing outside the bookshop last week. Harrison was waving some kind of paperwork at her, and Charlotte didn't look so calm that time."

Sam didn't want to consider that Charlotte might be involved in a murder. She considered her a friend. But she could understand how angry she'd apparently gotten over the situation she was in. "Sounds like Harrison enjoyed confrontations."

"He thrived on them," Diane said. "But Charlotte worried me that day. I'd never seen her lose her composure like that." She glanced across the yard where the golden retriever had finally flopped onto his side, surrounded by smaller dogs including Echo and Arlo. "When someone quiet finally snaps, it can be more dangerous than someone who's always vocal about their anger."

Sam thought about Charlotte's quiet determination in the bookstore earlier that day, calmly boxing up rare books even as her business sat damaged by floodwaters. The image of Charlotte's hand bleeding through a small bandage flashed in her mind.

"We all have our breaking points," Sam said.

"Don't we just," Diane agreed, watching as Echo rolled dramatically onto his back. "In school, I learned that pressure builds up silently until there's a catastrophic release. Nature or human nature, the principle's the same."

"You know," Diane said, watching Echo run excitedly in a tight circle, "if you're ever curious about the environmental work I do, you should stop by my monitoring station. It's in the old carriage house on Elm Street, which I converted last year. I've got some interesting documentation about how wildlife adapts to historic buildings."

"I'd like that," Sam replied, genuinely interested. "I've never thought about how environmental science intersected with architecture."

"More than most people realize," Diane said with a smile. "The bats at the hotel are a perfect example."

Ginny's call for everyone to try her "apocalypse brownies" interrupted them, and the conversation shifted to lighter topics as they joined the others around a folding table set up in the shade.

Ginny approached them with a wide smile. "Are you two solving the world's problems over here? Because the rest of us are just watching dogs act ridiculous and eating stale chips."

Sam laughed. "We're getting there. One environmental crisis at a time."

"Well, take a break and come watch Lucy's whippet try to figure out why Dave's border collie keeps herding him into a corner." Ginny grinned. "It's better than streaming TV, which is good because none of us have that right now anyway."

They moved to join the others, and Sam filed away the new information about Diane and the hotel's east side. The conversation shifted to storm stories and cleanup efforts as the dogs continued their joyful play in the yard.

After an hour of much-needed dog therapy and human connection, Sam felt her shoulders and jaw finally relaxing. Ginny had been right. She and Arlo needed this.

As they prepared to leave a little while later, Sam noticed Diane making notes in a small field journal.

"Still working, even during our break?" Sam asked.

Diane smiled ruefully. "Force of habit. I was just making a list of habitat sites I need to check tomorrow." She tucked the notebook away. "The storm has probably affected several protected areas. I'm planning to ask Angie Mills to help with the photography documentation. That girl has serious talent with a camera."

"Angie? Trevor's daughter?" Sam asked. She wouldn't have thought Diane would know the girl.

"Yes, she's been helping me document the bat habitats. Her actual senior project is architectural photography, but she's been generous with her time helping my research, too."

Which would explain how Angie had seemed so familiar with architecture at the clubhouse when Sam was looking at her pictures. Sam bent to clip Arlo's leash as he trotted over, his energy finally spent. "Small world. She walks Arlo for me sometimes."

"She's a remarkable kid," Diane said. "She's planning on heading to college next year. Though with all this damage, who knows what everyone's plans will look like now. I'd imagine some folks will need to put college on hold for a year."

As they said their goodbyes, Sam gave Ginny a grateful hug. "This was exactly what we all needed. Thank you."

Chapter Eleven

The sun was starting to lower in the sky as she and Arlo approached the house. She could see Nora on the porch with Precious. Arlo quickened his pace at the sight of his pit bull friend, eager to resume whatever canine friendship they'd established.

"There you are," Nora called as they approached. "I was beginning to think you'd been swept away by a secondary flood."

"Oh, it was just a mental health break. Ginny organized an impromptu dog social. Any updates from the clubhouse?"

Nora said, "Aiden called on the walkie-talkie. They've cleared most of the second entrance to the neighborhood. And there's a rumor that cell service might be partially restored by tomorrow morning."

"That would be helpful," Sam said.

Nora peered at her shrewdly. "You've got that look."

"What look?"

"The one where you're thinking too hard about something that's probably none of your business." Nora adjusted her glasses. "I've seen it before. Usually right before you end up in trouble."

Sam laughed. "I'm just processing everything that's happened today. It's been quite a day."

"Hmph," Nora responded, clearly unconvinced. "Well, process inside. Mrs. Fitzpatrick wants to know if you'll join our Scrabble tournament. We're playing for those fancy protein bars in your pantry."

As Sam followed Nora inside, she decided her investigation would have to wait until tomorrow. She'd play a little Scrabble with her guests before bowing out and turning in early.

Sam woke to the sound of heated debate. She blinked at the early morning sunlight filtering through her curtains, momentarily disoriented until she heard Mrs. Fitzpatrick's distinctive voice declaring that "J-A-R-L" was absolutely a word, and Nora's sharp retort that "made-up Viking titles" were not permitted in championship Scrabble.

Arlo, curled against her side, opened one eye and gave her a look that seemed to ask if they really had to get up and face whatever was happening in her living room. Sam sympathized completely.

"I know, buddy," she whispered, giving his ears a gentle scratch. "But hiding in here won't make them go away."

She padded to the bathroom, grateful that at least her master suite remained a guest-free zone. When she emerged dressed for the day, she found her dining room had been transformed into what appeared to be Scrabble Tournament Central. The table was covered with score sheets meticulously organized by round, player statistics were charted on a large piece of cardboard propped against her china cabinet, and someone had created a trophy out of an empty tuna can and aluminum foil.

"Good morning," Sam said, stepping carefully around Mr. Daniels, who was doing stretching exercises on her living room rug while Precious watched with what looked like professional disapproval.

"There she is!" Nora announced. "We decided to let you sleep through the quarterfinals. Mrs. Fitzpatrick is officially disqualified for attempting to use Norse mythology to score a triple word."

Mrs. Fitzpatrick looked unrepentant. "I maintain that a jarl is a type of Scandinavian nobleman, and therefore a perfectly legitimate word."

"The rules clearly state no titles of nobility," Nora countered, tapping a handwritten sheet of paper that had not existed yesterday evening.

Sam just nodded and smiled, then made her way to the kitchen, where she found her coffee already brewed. A note in Nora's precise handwriting informed her the generator was running at "94% efficiency" and that they had reorganized her spice rack "alphabetically, with emergency notations."

She wasn't entirely sure what an emergency notation for paprika might be, but decided that was a mystery for another day.

After checking that her senior guests had everything they needed and making a quick breakfast of oatmeal for herself and kibbles for Arlo, Sam grabbed her keys and emergency kit. "I'm going to check in at the clubhouse for a minute, then help Olivia with food distribution," she announced.

"Excellent," said Nora, not looking up from her Scrabble tiles. "We'll hold down the fort. I've paired Mrs. Fitzpatrick with Precious to even the playing field." She winked.

The pit bull, now sporting a bow tie that matched Nora's cardigan, thumped his tail once in acknowledgment.

"Don't worry about us," Mrs. Fitzpatrick added cheerfully. "We've found your emergency checklist for power outages. We're going to grade your preparation level while you're gone."

Sam managed a smile that she hoped didn't look as strained as it felt. "Looking forward to my score." As she headed for the door, Arlo trotting beside her, she heard the seniors already debating the point value of "Q" on their modified scoring system.

Sam drove to the clubhouse and stuck her head in to see if she was needed. Everything seemed to be working smoothly, though. She did see a note from Olivia on the whiteboard that the food distribution for the pantry had been moved to the community center, which had generator power. She hopped back in the car to help out there.

The drive to the community center took longer than it should have, with several detours around fallen trees and repair crews already hard at work. The center itself was a hub of activity when she arrived. Folding tables lined the walls, each stacked with different categories of supplies. Volunteers sorted donations while others assembled care packages.

Sam spotted Olivia near the loading dock, clipboard in hand, her auburn hair pulled back in a practical ponytail. Despite the chaos around her, she looked more energized than Sam had seen her in months. There was a new confidence in her posture as she directed volunteers.

"Need another pair of hands?" Sam asked.

Olivia's face lit up. "Sam! Perfect timing." She gestured toward a stack of printed maps on the table beside her. "We've got the south side neighborhoods covered, but we're still trying to reach Cedar Creek and Pinewood. The main roads are blocked, but Jason thinks he found an access point through the old hiking trail."

As if summoned by his name, Jason appeared, carrying a box of canned goods. Olivia's younger brother looked remarkably put together for someone who'd been delivering supplies since dawn, though his credit union golf shirt was now wrinkled and mud-splattered.

"Great to see you, Sam" he said, setting down the box. "Any chance your Type-A powers extend to mapping alternate delivery routes? The county guys keep telling me roads are impassable, but I refuse to believe there's not some way through."

"I might have a few ideas," Sam said, already examining the maps. "The old fire road behind Wellington Street might work if the creek hasn't overflowed."

"See? This is why we need her," Jason told his sister with a grin. "I'll load up the Jeep while you two catch up." He nodded toward a quieter corner of the gymnasium. "Olivia could use a five-minute break anyway. She's been here since five this morning. And all evening yesterday."

"I'm fine," Olivia protested, but Sam could see the fatigue behind her eyes.

"Five minutes," Sam said firmly, guiding her friend toward two folding chairs in a relatively quiet corner. "They can survive without you for five minutes."

Olivia sank into the chair with a sigh. "It's been non-stop. But in a good way, you know? People really come together in a crisis."

Sam nodded, watching as volunteers efficiently packed boxes and checked addresses. "You've got this place running like a well-oiled machine."

"It helps to focus on something." Olivia lowered her voice. "I heard about Harrison Blackwood from Jason. He was helping clear debris near the hotel and overheard the police. Is it true?"

Sam glanced around to ensure they weren't overheard. "Yes."

"Was it really the storm? That killed him, I mean?"

"That's what I've been trying to figure out," Sam admitted. "I've been talking to people who knew him."

Olivia leaned forward, her expression turning serious. "And?"

"And it seems like half the town had a reason to want him gone." Sam checked her watch, noting they still had a few minutes before Jason would be back. "Actually, I could use a sounding board. I've been gathering information, but I'm having trouble keeping it straight."

"Well," Olivia said, shifting into the practical, organized mode that had made them fast friends, "you've got five minutes and my undivided attention. Walk me through what you know so far."

"Okay," said Sam. "First off, I was with Kevin when we found Harrison. You might not have heard that."

"I knew you and Kevin were going to look for him. You're the ones who actually found him?"

"That's right. Harrison was outside and something about it all just seemed really off. There was a whole staged vibe."

Olivia said, "That's weird. So not so much a storm casualty."

"I mean, it could be. But it just seemed wrong."

Olivia said, "Kevin hasn't had the best time with Harrison, himself. Did he look like he was relieved Harrison was gone?"

"You know, I didn't even look at him to get a reaction. At the time, I was mostly focused on trying to get help, since we couldn't make any phone calls. But I've heard he and Harrison had real issues with each other. I know they'd been business partners in the past, and that it didn't work out."

Olivia nodded. "Kevin was saying he thought he'd been cheated out of previous deals. I don't know much about it, but I know he was mad." She tilted her head to one side. "I seem to remember Harrison had a problem with a university professor or something, too."

"That's right. Victor Reid. He's been upset with Harrison over his plans to demolish and develop local historic buildings, like the old library." Sam didn't mention the gambling. She didn't want to start any rumors, even though Olivia was a friend.

"That actually annoyed me, too. Sunset Ridge has some amazing old homes and other buildings. If a developer knocks them down and puts up cheap construction, we've lost something that makes the town unique." Olivia frowned. "Wait, didn't you tell me recently that Harrison approached *you*, too?"

"He sure did. I turned him down and sent him away, but he didn't take kindly to it. From time to time, he's called to see if I've reconsidered. I ended up blocking his phone number, actually."

Olivia made a face. "Well, I'm sorry he's dead, but he sounds like a real pain."

"Harrison rubbed people the wrong way, for sure."

Olivia asked, "Have we covered all the people who were upset with him?"

"Unfortunately, no. There's also Charlotte Webb."

"Oh, the bookshop lady downtown? I always thought she had the coolest name for the business she's in. I'm sure her parents named her that on purpose. She probably read *Charlotte's Web* a million times when she was a kid," said Olivia.

"Right? That's what I've always thought, too. And I really like her. But she was seriously unhappy with Harrison for trying to buy up shops downtown. She refused to sell and took out loans to improve the property so he couldn't claim the shop had blight." Sam also remembered again the bleeding cut on Charlotte's hand.

"That store has been in her family for generations, you know. I can't imagine downtown without the shop. And I can't imagine Charlotte doing anything else."

Sam said, "Me either. Then there's Diane Foster. Do you know her?"

"I've been at some get-togethers with her before. Let me guess. Harrison ran afoul of her environmental causes. That seems par for the course for a developer like him."

"Exactly. There are apparently some exotic bats in the old hotel he bought."

Olivia said, "Wait. Exotic bats?"

"Well, more like rare bats, I guess. Diane drew up an environmental impact study, which Harrison tried to cover up so he could move forward with some large-scale renovations at the hotel. Plus, Diane's dad would have lost parking spaces under his plans at his place."

Olivia said, "That's right, her dad owns the nature center. It's cute, if you haven't made it over there yet. It was made with kids in mind, but I love going there."

"I'll have to check it out."

Olivia said, "Is that everybody? And are we counting you in the mix?" She gave Sam a wink.

Sam laughed. "My aggravation with Harrison ended when I blocked his number. But we can keep me on the list if you want to remain open to possibilities. I didn't like him, that's for sure. There's one other person I haven't mentioned, though—Trevor Mills."

Olivia groaned. "Don't tell me my favorite contractor is a killer. I won't be able to stand it. He's the only builder in town I really trust. But I guess all the dots connect. Trevor's in the same industry as Harrison. It sounds like it would be tough to avoid dealing with him."

"All I know is that Trevor lost a major bid to an out-of-state company, even though he had the lower bid. He was mad that he'd invested a lot of money for the project and then didn't get it."

Olivia shook her head. "It's tough to believe any of those people would have murdered somebody, even someone like Harrison. They're all really well thought-of in the community, you know?"

"I guess we never know what can happen when someone is under a lot of pressure, though. It could make a person snap."

Olivia asked, "Do you think this was a spur-of-the-moment thing, then? Someone just lashed out? Or was it planned?"

"It didn't seem like it was something very well planned to me. But who knows? I do think whoever did it was hoping Harrison's death would be written off as a storm-related blunt-force trauma death."

A small smile tugged at the corner of Olivia's mouth. "You're starting to sound like a cop, Sam."

Sam made a face. "I probably watch too many crime dramas on TV. I don't think Aiden would say I'm anything *close* to being a cop."

"Ahh," said Olivia playfully. "Now we're getting on a subject that's close to my heart. Or, should I say, close to *your* heart. How are things with Aiden? Any progress there?" Then she gestured to a table with boxes of food. "Let's sort canned goods while you mull on that."

Sam followed Olivia over to the table. "I don't know, Olivia. I feel like I'm leading Aiden on a little. I've been burned before, as you know, so I'm trying to take things slow. Really slow. More like glacial. He's been great, too, trying hard not to push a relationship on me before I'm ready. I just wish the process was easier. I have a great time when we're together."

"Is there something holding you back? I'm not saying moving slow is necessarily a bad thing. You know what you need. But the man practically lights up when you walk into a room."

The question about what was holding Sam back hung in the air as they continued sorting supplies. Around them, volunteers moved with purpose, the routine of the food pantry providing a comforting rhythm amid the chaos the storm had left behind.

"I don't know, Liv," Sam finally said, her voice lower now. "After Chad, I keep expecting to find something wrong with

Aiden. I search for red flags even when there aren't any." She laughed, but without any real humor. "It's exhausting being this suspicious all the time."

Olivia paused her sorting, giving Sam her full attention. "That's what betrayal does to you. It's not your fault."

"I know that logically," Sam said, methodically aligning the cans in perfect rows. "But there's this voice in my head that keeps saying if I was fooled once, I could be fooled again. Chad seemed perfect too, remember? Right up until he wasn't."

"Aiden's not Chad," Olivia said gently, taking the can from Sam's hand and setting it down so Sam would look at her.

"No, he's not." Sam sighed. "But sometimes I wonder if I'll ever be able to trust my own judgment again. What if I'm permanently damaged in that way now?"

"You're not damaged, Sam. You're healing." Olivia squeezed her hand. "And healing isn't straightforward. Some days you'll feel ready to take risks, and other days you'll want to hide behind your lists and schedules."

Sam smiled ruefully. "You know me pretty well, don't you?"

"I've had front-row seats to your recovery, remember?" Olivia said. "And I know that underneath all those perfectly organized spreadsheets and emergency response plans is a woman with an enormous capacity for love." She reached for another box of donations. "Just don't let what Chad did rob you of that. He's taken enough already."

Sam nodded, feeling strangely lighter for having voiced her fears. "When did you get so wise?"

"Please, I've always been wise," Olivia laughed, her eyes crinkling at the corners. "You've just been too busy organizing the neighborhood's disaster response to notice."

They both chuckled.

Olivia, thankfully, quickly changed the subject. "Now tell me how things are going at your house? Or should I call it command central?"

Sam gave her friend a weary grin. "I'm hoping the clubhouse is command central, actually. But it's kind of hard to tell. Nora and the gang threw an all-night Scrabble tournament last night."

"You're kidding me."

Sam said, "Unfortunately not."

"Was it fueled by alcohol?"

Sam said, "I think it was fueled by chocolate. And a love of unusual words and arguing over Scrabble rules. Anyway, they're happy, the folks with medical needs seem to be doing well, and I'm glad I can help out." She glanced around. "Speaking of helping, run me through how things are going here at the food pantry."

"It's a makeshift food pantry, but it'll do. We've mostly got non-perishables, of course, but we do have a few fresh items that we're saving from spoiling by being moved to facilities with generators." Olivia gave a mock bow to Sam. "Like yours."

"Oh, it was my pleasure. So you've been able to get a generator here, obviously. Does that mean that everything for the food pantry is out of my house now? Or that my guests have eaten them all?"

Olivia laughed. "No, they haven't over-indulged. We got the food out of there as soon as we got this location set up."

"And Jason, with his four-wheel drive, is getting food to neighborhoods that have been cut-off?"

"Well, not totally cut off, but areas that are more challenging to get to because of mudslides. Jason can get so close, then he gets out, climbs over downed trees, and puts supplies in a central location for residents there." Olivia shrugged. "It's really the best we can do to get food quickly to different areas."

"Is there a way to handle the logistics? Track which neighborhoods have been served and who might have critical needs where? I know that has to be tricky with the cell towers and internet down."

They discussed the ins and outs of getting the best routes possible for a while.

Olivia handed Sam a box of canned vegetables to sort while they talked. The community center hummed with activity as volunteers organized donated supplies for distribution.

"You wouldn't believe how much food people have managed to share," Olivia said, wiping a strand of hair from her forehead. "Even with their own kitchens in shambles, they're bringing whatever they can spare."

Sam said, "I love hearing that. Everybody is going through a tough time, but folks are still pulling together."

A man walked in, looking a little lost. He apparently decided Olivia and Sam must be in charge, because he hurried over. "Hey there. I own Mike's BBQ downtown. I lost power, of course, and decided to grill everything before it went bad. My pickup out back is loaded with insulated food carriers. I've been up since dawn grilling this stuff. I wanted the emergency workers and power crews to get it. I figured you guys would know how to arrange that."

"Oh my gosh, this is fantastic," said Olivia.

"Hey, I was happy to do it. It didn't make any sense to let this meat go to waste. And the community has done a lot for me, so I thought I'd try to return the favor. There's pulled pork, grilled chicken, and some sides."

Sam and Olivia helped bring in the food, then thanked Mike again as he left. Olivia said, "This smells heavenly. But we're going to need to distribute it pretty quickly. We don't have the space here in the fridges to keep it. And it would be better warm, anyway."

"It would be great if we could let the local radio station know," said Sam. "I know people are listening on their emergency radios." She looked at her watch. "Tell you what. Let me run over to the station, if the roads aren't blocked. There's no other way to let them know right now."

"That would be great, if you could. And we've got more reinforcements coming here in thirty minutes, so don't worry about coming back if you've got other stuff to work on. I know you're doing a lot in the neighborhood, too."

"How about if I plan on swinging by, but if I get pulled away by something else, don't be too surprised," said Sam. She hurried off to her car to start wending her way to the radio station.

Chapter Twelve

Fortunately, Sam was able to drive to the station with only a few detours because of downed powerlines and trees. The DJ had been thrilled to make the announcement and said he'd direct the power crews and emergency workers to report to the staging area behind the community center where the utility trucks were parked.

Sam was heading back to the community center again when her walkie-talkie started chirping at her. It was Kevin Zhang.

"Hey, Sam. Sorry to bug you. I got your frequency from the emergency coordination list at the clubhouse. Have you seen Aiden around?"

"Not today, but I talked to him yesterday. Why, what's going on?"

Kevin hesitated. "I think I figured out something important. But I can't get hold of the cops. I thought I'd run it by Aiden, since he used to be a detective. The police are slammed right now with disaster recovery, and I don't want to bother them if it's not a big deal."

"Have you tried him on the walkie-talkie? He has one."

Kevin said, "Yeah, he's not picking up. He must be out of range. I know he was planning to help with road clearing today, on one of the main routes in."

"If you want, I can meet up with you, to be a sounding board. Where are you?"

"Back at the hotel," Kevin said. "There's no hurry. It's probably nothing."

Sam considered this. "Okay. I was heading to the community center, so let me turn around. I'll be right there."

"Sure, no rush. Take your time."

She drove carefully, still skirting debris in the roads. The rain had picked up again, too, which didn't make driving any easier. When she finally reached the hotel, Sam hopped out of her car and looked for Kevin, wishing she'd asked him if he was going to be inside or outside of the hotel, because he was nowhere in sight.

Sam called Kevin's name, but there was no answer. The whole place seemed very quiet, and it looked as though the guests at the hotel had left and somehow found an open route to get back to wherever they lived. But then, it couldn't be much fun staying somewhere with no power. All of the businesses were closed and there couldn't be trails open with so many trees down.

The light rain picked up more, and Sam zipped up her windbreaker. "Kevin?" she called again, wondering if he'd gone inside to escape the rain. She did see his Pathfinder in the parking lot.

Sam walked inside and asked the woman at the front desk if she'd seen Kevin. She shook her head.

Sam frowned as she headed back outside again. She hadn't been long, and Kevin was supposed to be expecting her. She hesitated, then walked around the side of the hotel, near where Harrison was found.

Sam stopped short when she spotted a figure lying on the ground below the scaffolding.

Chapter Thirteen

Sam, shaking, walked up to the figure. It was Kevin. She blew out a breath, closing her eyes for a second, not wanting to see him like this. Then she swiftly reached down to check for a pulse, but there was nothing.

Sam tried to call the police channel on the walkie-talkie, but there was only static.

Kevin lay crumpled on the ground below the east wing scaffolding, his body positioned in a way that made her stomach turn. No one collapsed naturally like that. A small crater in the muddy ground marked where he'd landed.

She looked up at the scaffolding above, then back at Kevin. With his distance from the building and the angle of his fall, there was no question he'd come from the roof.

Sam heard a car door behind her and hurried back to the parking lot to see a construction worker in a pickup truck arriving. She flagged him over. "Have you seen the police out anywhere this morning? There's been a murder."

The worker looked flabbergasted. "What? Here at the hotel?"

"Yes. Could you please find someone who can help? I'm going to stay and protect the scene."

Wordlessly, the man climbed back into his truck and took off.

Sam turned to sadly look at Kevin again. He was crumpled on the ground, and she felt an urge to walk over and cover him up somehow. But she stayed where she was, straining to see from a distance if there was any physical evidence. She noticed footprints in the mud, and hoped those would eventually help the police make an arrest. Finally, she heard sirens in the distance, coming closer.

At first, it was a uniformed cop, looking terse. Sam pointed to Kevin, and the young man walked swiftly over to the scene. He also checked for a pulse and, finding none, got on his radio. Then he stood sentry over the body until Bill Hawkins, the police chief, arrived. The chief looked exhausted and none too pleased that Sam had discovered another body. And that the body was her co-discoverer of the first body.

Chief Hawkins took control of the scene, swiftly getting the uniformed cop to set up crime scene tape and document the scene with photographs since the light rain had gotten heavier. "Until forensics can get here," he barked.

The chief seemed very curt, which didn't surprise Sam. After all, this was very clearly a crime scene, as opposed to the ambivalence surrounding Harrison's death. He walked up to her. "Can you tell me how you ended up on the scene?"

"Kevin called me on my walkie-talkie to see if I knew where Aiden was," said Sam.

Hawkins leaned in. "Aiden? You mean Aiden Wood?"

"That's right. Kevin couldn't get in touch with the police, and he said he wanted to bounce something off Aiden, since he'd been in the force. But I didn't know Aiden's location, so I told Kevin I'd meet him here so he could use me as a sounding board."

"And he was dead when you arrived?"

Sam said, "Well, I couldn't find him, which I thought was strange, since he knew I was coming over. I walked inside to see if he was waiting indoors because of the rain. But they hadn't seen him in there. So I walked around the side of the building."

"He's very close to where Harrison was," said Chief Hawkins. There was a hard note in his voice as he studied Sam.

Sam gave him a calm look back. "Kevin is. But I had nothing to do with his death, nor Harrison's." She paused. "Have you learned whether Harrison's death was homicide or not?"

Hawkins was quiet for a few moments, then said, "It was. Which makes the whole thing pretty odd, in my way of thinking. And it's very coincidental that you're at both scenes."

Sam's first reaction was to be defensive, but she thought that might not play well with the police chief. "It is, yes. But it's just circumstance."

Hawkins rubbed his forehead as he considered the scene. Then he said slowly, "From what I hear around town, it sounds like you ran into some trouble with Harrison."

"Trouble? That's a bit overstated. Harrison was interested in buying my home and property for a development he was considering. I didn't want to sell. That was the end of the story."

Hawkins nodded, but his eyes were still hard. "Got it. Except maybe it wasn't the end of the story for Harrison, right?

He was a fellow who liked getting his way, as I recall. I heard he might have been talking smack about you behind your back. Stuff like that."

"Which was irritating and childish but hardly a reason for me to want to kill him."

Hawkins apparently decided to leave it there. "Okay. Did Kevin give you a hint as to what he'd found out?"

"Nothing," said Sam, wishing again she'd kept him on the phone.

He gave a curt nod. "What were you doing last night and this morning?"

"Last night? I spoke to Kevin just minutes ago."

"Regardless of that," said Hawkins.

Sam said, "Last night, I had seniors in my house playing a Scrabble tournament. My generator is working, so they're there with oxygen and other medical equipment."

"They can confirm that?"

"Absolutely," said Sam. "They were there all night. I went to sleep, and they stayed up playing the game."

"Okay," said Hawkins. "I might have more questions later, so don't be surprised if I stop by." And with that, he stomped away.

Sam was just leaving the hotel grounds, the police activity still buzzing behind her, when she spotted Trevor Mills talking with a uniformed officer at the perimeter tape. His work truck was parked at an angle on the street, tools visible in the back under a tarp that flapped in the wind. The contractor's usually steady hands were gesturing emphatically as he spoke.

As she approached, the officer nodded and moved away, leaving Trevor staring at the hotel with a troubled expression.

"Trevor?" Sam called.

He turned. "Sam. I heard there was another death. Is it true?"

"I'm afraid so," she replied, lowering her voice. "Kevin Zhang."

Trevor's expression darkened. "This isn't just storm casualty stuff anymore, is it?"

"The police are investigating."

"The whole thing seems really off," Trevor said, running a hand through his hair. "First Harrison, now Kevin? Both of them connected to that hotel renovation? That's a real coincidence, right?"

Sam noticed the tension in his shoulders, the way his normally measured movements seemed hurried. "Are you okay? You seem worried about something beyond the obvious."

Trevor hesitated, then sighed. "I'm trying to find Angie. We were supposed to meet at the Johnson house at 7:30, but she never showed. It's really unlike her. She was going to document the damage for insurance claims. With communications down, I've been driving to all the places I thought she might be."

"When did you last see her?" Sam asked, noticing how Trevor kept scanning the area, as if his daughter might appear at any moment.

"First thing this morning. We've been getting up before dawn, though. Angie was still asleep when I headed out. She was planning to load up her camera gear and meet me at the site." His eyes returned to the hotel.

"I'm sure she's fine," Sam reassured him. "The roads are still a mess, and she could be stuck somewhere with no way to let you know."

Trevor nodded, though the worry didn't leave his eyes. "I know. I just can't stand the thought of her in any danger. Now it looks like both Harrison and Kevin might have been killed. They were obviously on their own early in the morning. What if Angie saw something or took a picture of something while she was out? The killer might have thought he had to shut her up."

"I'm sure she's okay," said Sam gently. "She probably just lost track of time."

He suddenly changed the subject, maybe not wanting to dwell on the possibility of something having happened to his only child. He gestured toward the hotel. "Did you know Kevin well?"

"Pretty well, yes. He seemed like a good father, very protective of Emma. We weren't close, but I respected how much he cared about his daughter." Sam somberly thought how horrible it was going to be for Gemma to learn of her father's death. She was just a child.

"Actually," Trevor said, frowning slightly, "I saw Kevin yesterday afternoon at the hotel. He was examining something on the east side scaffolding, taking photos with his phone. When he noticed me, he put away the phone quickly. He seemed kind of rattled that someone had spotted him."

"Did he say what he was looking at?" Sam asked.

Trevor shook his head. "No, but he was focused on the roofline. He wasn't with his regular assessment team. It struck me as odd at the time." He paused. "I wouldn't have been surprised if Kevin had somehow been involved with Harrison's death. He had his issues with Harrison, after all. Their business relationship didn't end well."

"So I heard," Sam said, watching Trevor's reaction.

Trevor's expression hardened. "Harrison made plenty of enemies. And of course, he gave that hotel renovation contract to an out-of-state company. I'd told you about that. It cost me a lot, both financially and reputation-wise." His hands tightened into fists before consciously relaxing them.

"The renovation contract meant a lot to you," Sam observed.

"It would have funded Angie's college," Trevor admitted. "I'd invested in specialized equipment for the historical work to give me a leg up." Trevor's expression hardened. "And Harrison didn't just reject my bid—he humiliated me in front of the historical preservation board. He called my methods 'quaint but obsolete.' Harrison thought modern construction had no place for 'sentimental craftsmanship.' Three generations of Mills men have restored buildings in this town. My grandfather taught me how to hand-cut joinery for those cornices Harrison was so eager to tear down."

He caught himself, taking a deep breath. "Sorry. It still gets to me. That contract wasn't just about money, you know? It was about respect for this town's history." He rubbed his face. "This stuff gets me really worked up. Anyway, that's not important now. I need to find my daughter."

"Could she have gone to the community center? A lot of volunteers are coordinating there," Sam suggested.

Before Trevor could answer, a truck pulled up beside them. Alfred Jones leaned out the window, his burly frame instantly recognizable.

"Trevor! There you are," Alfred called. "I just saw Angie up at the high school. She's helping Aiden set up that charging station you were talking about."

Relief washed over Trevor's face. "She's okay? You're sure it was her?"

"Definitely," Alfred confirmed. "She was hauling in batteries when I dropped off some extension cords. She said her car battery died at your house and she walked over to her boyfriend's house, and he gave her a ride in his truck. She asked me to let you know, and I've been trying to find you to tell you."

Trevor's shoulders sagged with relief. "Thanks, Alfred."

As Alfred drove away, Trevor turned back to Sam. "I was probably overreacting, but with everything happening, it scared me."

"That's totally understandable," Sam assured him.

Trevor's expression shifted, becoming more serious. "Going back to what we were talking about, there's somebody else that wasn't crazy about Harrison. Victor Reid."

"Victor? Why?" Sam asked, though she already had her suspicions.

"He's somebody else I saw at the hotel yesterday. Kevin was during the day, but Victor was here late last night," Trevor said, lowering his voice. "He was just standing in the rain, staring at the building. When I called out, he took off." Trevor glanced around before continuing. "His gambling's gotten worse since he lost his job. Everyone knows he blames Harrison for that.

And he knew every detail of that hotel's structure—every weakness, every architectural element."

"That's interesting," Sam said, filing away the information. "I didn't realize he'd been at the hotel recently." In fact, Victor had talked about how he'd been staying in the old library without even really poking his head outside. Maybe he'd finally gotten tired of being holed up, but it seemed strange he'd have chosen to go to the hotel and late at night.

"Victor is desperate," Trevor continued. "I've known him for years and helped him restore some of the historical buildings. But he's not himself. The pressure's getting to him. The gambling has been bad. I heard he lost five thousand at an online poker game last month. Five thousand he doesn't have."

"Did he blame Harrison for his financial troubles?" Sam asked.

"Sure. He told anyone who'd listen that Harrison had ruined him. He also mentioned there'd be 'consequences' for destroying the town's heritage." Trevor's expression grew troubled. "I thought it was just talk at the time."

Sam said, "Everything looks different now, doesn't it? I should let you get back," she said. "I'm glad Angie's okay."

Chapter Fourteen

After parting ways with Trevor, Sam felt the weight of the morning's events pressing down on her. Two deaths, both connected to the hotel, and a police chief who clearly suspected her involvement. It definitely wasn't a good start to the day. Suddenly, she felt exhausted. The light rain had intensified, and she pulled her jacket tighter as she hurried back to her car.

She sat still behind the wheel for a moment. She knew she'd mentioned going back to the community center, but she suddenly didn't feel like being around that many people. Olivia had told her she had everything covered with volunteers, after all. Sam considered going back home, but her mind was spinning after Kevin's death, and she didn't particularly want to be social with her guests there.

She thought she'd run by Charlotte's bookshop again. The store was right down the street. Maybe Charlotte had seen or heard something. Since the rain was picking up, she decided to try to park on Main Street instead of walking over.

The downtown area looked marginally better than it had a couple of days ago, though that wasn't saying much. Work crews had cleared the main thoroughfares of the largest debris, creating neat piles of branches, roofing materials, and twisted metal at regular intervals along the street. The floodwaters had receded further, leaving behind a thick layer of mud that was slowly drying in patches where the rain wasn't reaching.

She noticed Charlotte had managed to get a blue tarp secured over the damaged portion of her roof. The cracked front window had been boarded up with plywood, on which someone had painted "Still Open" in bright yellow letters. The shop's hanging sign had been rehung properly, though it still creaked in the light wind. Several milk crates full of water-damaged books sat under an overhang with a handwritten sign: "Free: Damp but Readable."

The bell above the door gave a more confident jingle than it had day-before-yesterday as Sam pushed it open. Inside, the transformation was remarkable. The mud line was still visible about three feet up the walls, but Charlotte had clearly been working non-stop. The floors were mopped clean, though still damp in places. Dehumidifiers hummed in each corner, powered by a small generator that sat just outside the back door. Books had been carefully organized on higher shelves, with empty lower shelves now wrapped in plastic sheeting as protection against any future water incursion.

Charlotte was on a stepladder, carefully wiping down book spines with a cloth that smelled of some kind of preservative. Her dark brown hair was tied back in a bandana, and she wore work gloves to protect her hands. When she spotted Sam, her exhausted face brightened.

"Sam! I didn't expect to see you back so soon." She climbed down from the ladder, pulling off one glove to push her wire-rimmed glasses up her nose. "How are things at your place?"

"It's chaotic but manageable," Sam replied, looking around the shop with genuine admiration. "Charlotte, this is incredible. You've made so much progress since day-before-yesterday."

Charlotte looked around her shop with a mixture of pride and weariness. "Amazing what you can accomplish when you can't sleep and don't have a TV to distract you." She gestured to a group of high school students sorting books in the back. "I've had some wonderful volunteers. The kids from the high school English club showed up this morning to help. They've been absolute lifesavers."

She lowered her voice. "And thank you again for taking those rare books. I've been having anxiety dreams about water damage destroying the first edition Faulkner." She pointed to the now-empty rare book cabinet behind the register. "That collection represents my retirement plan, such as it is."

"They're perfectly safe," Sam assured her. "I've got them elevated in my sunroom, which stayed completely dry."

"Can I offer you some tea? It's just lukewarm, I'm afraid. The generator doesn't have enough power for the kettle." Charlotte held up a thermos.

"That would be wonderful, actually." Sam accepted the offer, realizing she hadn't had anything to drink since the night before.

Charlotte poured the tea into two mismatched mugs and led Sam to the small reading nook in the corner, now cleared of debris and featuring two relatively clean armchairs. Through the window, they could see people walking purposefully through town, carrying supplies or helping with cleanup efforts.

"So," Charlotte said, settling into one of the chairs with a sigh. "What brings you back to my humble, semi-flooded establishment?"

Sam took a sip of the tea, gathering her thoughts. The warmth of the mug was comforting against her cold hands. She noticed Charlotte's hand wore an adhesive bandage, the white edge just visible beneath her work glove.

"How's your hand doing?" Sam asked, nodding toward it.

Charlotte glanced down. "Oh, much better. One of my neighbors is a nursing student. She cleaned it properly and said I didn't need stitches after all." She flexed her fingers cautiously. "Just a hazard of clearing broken glass, I'm afraid. Now, what's on your mind? You have that look."

"What look?" Sam asked, echoing her earlier conversation with Nora.

"The one that says you're organizing information," Charlotte said with a small smile. "I recognize it because I do the same thing when I'm cataloging a complicated collection."

Sam took a deep breath. "I'm afraid there's been another death. Kevin Zhang was found murdered at the hotel this morning."

Charlotte's face paled at the news. She set her mug down with a trembling hand. "Kevin? But he was just here yesterday afternoon."

Sam straightened. "He was here at your shop?"

"He came by asking what I knew about the hotel's history. Specifically about the east wing. He seemed really interested in the rooftop finials. He wanted to know everything I knew about the original pieces. He kept asking if I was sure about how many there used to be."

"Did he say why?"

Charlotte hesitated. "He mentioned something about 'interference with historical integrity.' Kevin said he'd found evidence someone had removed original features from the hotel."

Sam recalled the missing element in the roofline that had caught her attention. "What kind of features?"

Charlotte leaned against the counter, her expression thoughtful. "The reason I know so much about the Ridgeview is because of my family. My great-aunt Millie worked at that hotel back in the day. She started there in 1952 when she was just sixteen. She always talked about those beautiful cast iron decorations along the roofline."

"Those are the finials?" asked Sam.

"That's right. Aunt Millie said they were original to the building and were 1890s Victorian work." Charlotte's expression grew troubled. "Kevin said his insurance photos didn't match what should be there. Some of those finials were missing, and he couldn't figure out why. The poor man seemed really upset about it. And Aunt Millie would have been heartbroken to know someone was stealing pieces of her old workplace."

Charlotte stood, frowning at one of the bookshelves. Then, nodding to herself, she pulled out a book and handed it to Sam. It was *The Ridgeview Hotel: A Photographic History*.

"This came out in the 90s with a limited print run to celebrate the hotel's centennial. Take a look at the photos of the roof," said Charlotte.

Sam studied pictures throughout the book. "They're really elaborate, aren't they?"

"Very Victorian," said Charlotte. "Kevin was particularly focused on this one." She showed Sam a close-up of an ornate finial with a distinctive leaf pattern. "The east corner piece—the most valuable one. It was gone when Kevin took his insurance photos."

"Someone's been stealing them," Sam said.

"It looks that way. And the timing matters." Charlotte pulled out maintenance records. "The scaffolding was put up just a few weeks ago to help with the hotel renovation."

Sam studied the photographs. "Did Kevin mention who he suspected?"

"He didn't." Charlotte gathered the photos. "Of course, Victor Reid has been documenting the hotel extensively. Trevor Mills had access through his restoration work. But honestly, anyone involved with the historical society or building would know which elements were valuable."

Sam settled back into her chair. "Charlotte, I'm sorry, but I need to ask. Where were you this morning before I arrived?"

Charlotte blinked, then understanding dawned. "You're asking for my alibi." She didn't seem offended. "I've been here at the shop since dawn. Mrs. Jenkins from the bakery brought pastries for the volunteers around seven. She'll confirm I was already here, covered in mud. I managed to get cleaned up with some paper towels before you arrived."

"You think Kevin's death is connected to Harrison's, don't you?" Charlotte's voice was quiet.

"I do. And I think both are connected to those missing finials." Sam leaned forward. "These finials, are they heavy enough to be used as weapons?"

Charlotte's eyes widened as the implication hit her. "Absolutely."

Sam rose to leave. "Could I take a couple of pictures of the hotel photographs?"

"Of course. Just be careful, Sam."

Sam nodded, understanding Charlotte's unspoken concern. "I'll watch my step."

A few minutes later, Sam climbed back into her car. She'd intended on going back to the community center to help out Olivia. But finding Kevin had left her head spinning. Instead, she spent the rest of the day at home with her guests and checking in now and then at the clubhouse. The image of Kevin's body kept intruding on her thoughts, making it difficult to focus even on Nora's continued Scrabble commentary. She made an early dinner for everyone, updated her investigation notes in private, and went to bed hoping tomorrow would bring some clarity.

Chapter Fifteen

The next morning, Sam woke to unusual quiet. A note on the kitchen counter in Nora's precise handwriting explained: *Community center medical facility operational. Relocated at dawn to secure optimal arrangements. Tournament semifinals commence at 9 AM sharp. - N*

Sam smiled despite herself. Even in an evacuation, Nora maintained her priorities.

The kitchen showed signs of the seniors' departure—they'd left it cleaner than they'd found it, with a note from Mrs. Fitzpatrick thanking Sam for the "hurricane hospitality" and promising to bring a homemade pie once the power returned. Beside it sat a small basket of defrosted muffins with another note explaining they were from the Hendersons, thanking her for letting them charge their devices.

Sam smiled, touched by the gesture, and took one of the banana nut muffins before heading to check on the generator.

Out of habit and not really expecting any messages, Sam checked her cell phone. Although there was currently no signal, it looked as if it had come back at some point earlier. There was a text from Lisa, Franklin's mom, sent around 6 AM: *Called in for emergency shift. Had to drop Franklin at community center early. Can you pick him up when convenient? Angie can babysit but not until 10. Will text when my shift ends. Thanks!*

Sam wasn't able to text back, of course, but made a mental note to try her connection at the community center in case the signal was better there. Then she grabbed her keys and headed out the door. It would be good to check on how the seniors were settling in anyway. Arlo gave her a meaningful look, and she scooped up the small dog to take him with her.

When Sam arrived inside, she was greeted by the familiar sounds of heated debate. Following the voices, she discovered Nora had established a Scrabble command post, complete with tournament brackets drawn on a whiteboard.

"Triple word score!" Mrs. Fitzpatrick declared triumphantly, placing her tiles on the board with a flourish. "That's 42 points."

Nora adjusted her glasses, scrutinizing the play. "I'm afraid 'QUIXOTIC' requires verification according to rule 17-B of our emergency Scrabble procedures."

"Hi Nora," Sam said, glancing around the room. "Everybody settling in okay here?"

"Fine and dandy."

Sam nodded. "I'm supposed to pick up Franklin and take him to meet his sitter. Is he with you?"

"Ah, yes," Nora said, momentarily distracted from her Scrabble arbitration. "Franklin got bored watching these amateurs play," Nora continued, making it clear who she considered the only true Scrabble expert in the room. "He wandered away." She frowned. "As a matter of fact, I haven't seen him in a while."

"He left a note," Mrs. Fitzpatrick added, holding up a scrap of paper with childish handwriting visible beneath her neatly penciled numbers. "Oh, was this important? I thought it was scratch paper for scoring."

Sam took the paper, making out Franklin's hastily scrawled message beneath the Scrabble scores: *Going outside. Back soon. —Franklin*

"How long ago was this?" Sam asked.

Nora consulted her own timepiece. "Well, it couldn't have been *that* long. Twenty minutes? Thirty?"

Sam moved to the rear windows, which overlooked playground equipment. The storm had transformed the area. The swing sets were damaged and benches were overturned. She could see no sign of Franklin in the immediate area.

"Franklin?" she called, heading through the back doors.

No response. She wasn't worried—Franklin was responsible for his age, but she needed to get him over to Angie and Trevor's house for babysitting.

"Franklin?" she called again, following a path toward a small wooded area that separated the playground from a retention pond. That's when Arlo took off running joyfully ahead of her.

Sam heard Arlo's distinctive bark, followed by a child's laughter. Following the sounds, she rounded a bend in the path to find an unexpected sight.

In a clearing where the trees had provided some shelter from the storm, Franklin had created an elaborate makeshift agility course. Using fallen branches, a section of the field's chain-link fence, and what looked like parts of a playground slide, he had constructed hurdles, weave poles, and even a tunnel from a blue tarp stretched over curved branches.

Arlo seemed to know exactly what to do. He darted through the tarp tunnel, emerging with his tail wagging furiously as Franklin cheered.

"That's it, Arlo!" Franklin called. "Good boy!"

Sam leaned against a tree, watching the scene with a smile. Franklin had replicated several of the standard agility obstacles with impressive ingenuity. The boy's face was flushed with excitement as he guided Arlo through the course again.

"I see you've been paying attention at agility class," Sam said, finally announcing her presence.

Franklin spun around, his expression momentarily guilty before breaking into a grin when he saw Sam wasn't upset. "I used the fallen branches from the storm. I made sure nothing was too heavy for even small dogs to jump over."

"I can see that," Sam said, impressed despite herself. "You've got a good eye for course design. But your mom texted me. She asked me to bring you over to Angie, who'll watch you until your mom's shift is over."

"Okay. Maybe Angie can hang out with me here. Do you think the course is good? I was taking notes last time we went to agility class," he added proudly, holding up his small notebook. "I drew diagrams of all the obstacles."

They watched as Arlo took another run through the course. Franklin said, "Arlo remembers everything. He's so smart."

Arlo, hearing his name, trotted over to Sam, his small body quivering with excitement from the exercise.

"I meant to stay where Miss Nora could see me, since she said she was responsible for me," Franklin explained as he began gathering his things. "But I found this perfect spot where the storm didn't knock everything down."

"It's a great spot," Sam acknowledged, impressed by Franklin's resourcefulness.

Franklin grinned. "I'll have to show Miss Nora the course. Maybe I can teach Precious some agility moves too."

Sam couldn't help laughing. "I'm sure Nora would love to see Precious navigating an agility course in his tutu."

"Do you think we could bring some of the other dogs here to practice?" Franklin asked, eyes lighting up at the possibility. "Maybe Lucy's whippet and Dave's border collie?"

"That's actually not a bad idea. A little normal activity might be good for everyone. Ginny had the dogs over to her yard to run around a couple of days ago, but there was no agility course there." She glanced at her watch. "Right now, though, we need to head out. I have to drop you off."

"Do you think it's okay for me to keep the course up for right now? It's pretty much out of the way of the community center stuff."

It certainly was. Sam considered this. "Well, I can't think that any normal activities are taking place out here anyway right now, considering the circumstances. How about if you leave it up for now and maybe you or your mom can call the parks and rec people to ask their permission later?"

Sam made a mental note to talk to the agility club about Franklin's makeshift training area. With the regular field damaged, this could become a temporary solution for the group. Plus, she knew Franklin would love to show off his work.

"Ready to go?" she asked as Franklin tucked his notebook into his pocket.

"Ready," Franklin replied, giving his course one last proud look.

After dropping Franklin at Angie's house and Arlo back home, Sam suddenly wanted to talk with Aiden. They hadn't talked since she'd found Kevin yesterday, and she wondered if he'd even heard the news. Of course, he was often in contact with his old friends at the police station, but with cell phones being up and down and as busy as both the police and Aiden had been, he might not be aware that Kevin had been murdered. She drove over to the high school to see if he was over there, and immediately spotted his car in the parking lot. The building had weathered the storm remarkably well, and now served as one of the town's main disaster response hubs. Generators hummed outside, powering essential services while teams of volunteers sorted supplies in the gymnasium.

Sam found Aiden in the former teacher's lounge. He was deep in conversation with several volunteers when he spotted her.

"Sam," he said, his expression brightening despite the exhaustion evident in his eyes. He excused himself from the group and crossed the room to meet her. "How are you?"

For a second, Aiden's kind eyes almost made her break down. She swallowed and said, "Well, it's been a little rough the past day. Did you hear about Kevin?"

He shook his head, but picked up something in Sam's tone. He glanced around at the bustling volunteers. "Let's find somewhere quieter to talk."

He led her to his classroom down the hall. Papers and emergency plans covered his desk, and a two-way radio crackled with intermittent updates from other coordination sites.

"You look like you've been busy," Sam commented as he cleared a stack of papers from a chair for her.

"I'm trying to keep up," Aiden admitted, rubbing the back of his neck. "The state emergency teams arrived this morning, but they're focusing on the downtown flooding. We're handling neighborhood coordination." He settled into his desk chair. "But I'm guessing you didn't come here to discuss my disaster management skills." His eyes searched her features. "Something's happened," Aiden said, studying her expression as he cleared a stack of papers from a chair. "I can see it in your face."

Sam sat down heavily. "Kevin Zhang is dead. I found his body at the hotel yesterday morning."

Aiden went very still. "What?"

"Someone pushed him from the roof. He'd called me on the walkie-talkie, and said he'd found something important about Harrison's death." Her voice was steadier than she felt. "When I got there, he was already gone."

Aiden ran a hand through his hair, then moved his desk chair to face her directly. "Are you okay? That's two bodies in just a few days."

"I keep seeing him lying there. Someone shoved him from the roof and just left him."

Aiden pulled his desk chair close enough that she could see the worry in his eyes. "Sam, that's traumatic for anyone."

She rubbed her temples. "The last twenty-four hours has kind of been a blur since I got that walkie-talkie call from Kevin."

"What exactly did he say when he called?"

Sam recounted Kevin's request to meet, his mention of finding something important, his inability to reach the police. "He sounded excited, like he'd figured something out. He'd wanted to speak with you about it, but couldn't reach you. I offered to come by so he could bounce ideas off me. I guess he must have known something."

"And then someone killed him for it," Aiden finished quietly.

"I've been trying to understand what Kevin might have discovered. Charlotte Webb gave me helpful background about the hotel's history and let me take pictures of a book she has."

Aiden's expression shifted from personal concern to professional interest as Sam showed him the historical photos. "Tell me what you found."

She pulled out her notebook where she'd written down what Charlotte had told her. "Charlotte's great-aunt used to work there, so she knows the history." Sam flipped through her notes. "Those decorative pieces on the roofline are called finials, and they're cast iron, zinc-coated ornaments. Charlotte said they're valuable to collectors and historically protected."

Sam handed her phone to Aiden so he could see the pictures from Charlotte's book on the hotel.

Sam continued, "Kevin had mentioned to Charlotte that some finials were missing from his recent insurance photos. Each one is about twenty pounds, according to the book she had. The zinc coating leaves distinctive marks, metallic gray with bluish-white edges, if you handle them."

Aiden's eyes sharpened. "Weren't there some distinctive marks on Harrison's body?"

"Exactly. Zinc oxidation leaves marks like the ones Kevin noticed on Harrison's clothing," Sam confirmed.

Aiden leaned back, processing this information. "So Kevin was investigating the missing rooftop decorations, discovered their connection to Harrison's death, and then was killed before he could share what he found."

"That seems possible. He told Charlotte he'd found evidence of someone stealing the ornaments. He assumed it was Harrison."

"I guess Harrison was creating his own supply of black-market architectural salvage," Aiden mused. "That's got to be a lucrative business for the right buyers. There's something else I learned today that connects these finials more directly to Harrison's death."

"What's that?" Sam asked.

"I spoke with my contact at the medical examiner's office. The wound measurements match the dimensions of these finials exactly. That distinctive leaf pattern would explain the ornate impression they found. And even the smaller decorative pieces weigh fifteen to twenty pounds of solid cast iron. That's easily enough to cause fatal injuries."

"So our killer needed access to the roof and knowledge of which finial was valuable," Sam said.

Aiden nodded.

Sam said, "The question is, who else knew about this? Who had the expertise to remove the finials, the knowledge of their value, and access to the hotel?"

"Which brings us to Victor Reid," Aiden said. "My former coworkers at the police department have been sharing concerns about him. His gambling debts are worse than people knew, and he's been acting increasingly erratic."

"Trevor mentioned seeing Victor at the hotel late at night," Sam added, recalling her earlier conversation. "And he also brought up concerns about Victor's gambling."

Aiden checked his watch. "Why don't you come along with me to visit him again? If he asks, we can say you were interested to hear more about your historic house."

"Do you think he's dangerous?" Sam asked quietly.

"Victor doesn't strike me as the careful, calculating type. But, of course, desperate people sometimes take risks."

"He definitely had motive," Sam acknowledged. "Harrison cost him his job, his home, his reputation. And he obviously has the knowledge to identify valuable architectural elements."

Aiden gathered his jacket from the back of his chair. "We should head over there. But Sam," he paused, his voice softening. "Be careful. If Victor is our killer, I don't want him seeing you as a threat."

Their eyes met, and for a moment, the professional distance between them dissolved. Sam felt that familiar flutter that she'd been trying to ignore since moving to Sunset Ridge. After Chad, she'd sworn off relationships entirely. But something about Aiden was different. His concern wasn't controlling. It seemed born of genuine care.

"I'm always careful," she replied with a small smile.

"That's debatable," Aiden said, the corner of his mouth quirking up. "Finding two murder victims in three days isn't exactly keeping a low profile."

As they walked to the parking lot, Sam filled Aiden in on what she'd learned the day before. She told him about how Harrison had been pressuring Charlotte to sell her bookstore and that she'd taken out loans to fight him off. She explained Diane's environmental monitoring permit that gave her access to the hotel, and Trevor's financial troubles after losing the renovation contract to Harrison's out-of-state company.

The old library came into view as they rounded the corner, its Victorian architecture imposing despite the storm damage surrounding it. A large oak had fallen against one side, and tarps covered sections of the roof where shingles had been torn away.

"Looks like Victor has been doing some emergency repairs," Aiden observed, nodding toward a ladder propped against the building.

The library's grand entrance was partially blocked by fallen branches that had been neatly stacked to one side.

Aiden knocked firmly on the heavy wooden door. Hearing no answer, Aiden cautiously opened the front door, which was unlocked.

Chapter Sixteen

"Victor?" Aiden called, his voice echoing in the cavernous space.

There was a crash from upstairs, followed by cursing. A moment later, Victor appeared at the railing, looking even more disheveled than during their last visit. His shirt was rumpled, his hair standing in various directions, and his wire-rimmed glasses sat slightly askew on his nose. Dark circles under his eyes suggested he hadn't slept in days.

"Aiden, Sam," he greeted them, his voice hoarse. "Please, come up. Excuse the mess."

As they climbed the stairs to his living space, Sam noticed water damage staining one corner of the ceiling.

Victor's makeshift living quarters looked more chaotic and more desperate than they had before. A sleeping bag lay unrolled in one corner, surrounded by stacks of books that formed makeshift walls. Empty liquor bottles were visible behind one stack.

Sam noticed several architectural drawings spread across a table. They appeared to be detailed plans of the Ridgeview House hotel, with the east wing circled repeatedly in red marker.

Victor followed her gaze and quickly gathered the papers, shuffling them into a messy pile.

"Research," he said with a nervous laugh. "Always more research to do."

"Victor," Aiden said, his tone gentle but direct. "Did you hear about Kevin Zhang?"

Victor's head jerked up. "Kevin? What about him?"

"He's dead," Sam said simply, watching Victor's reaction.

The blood drained from Victor's face. "Dead? Kevin's dead too?" He sank onto a wooden crate, his legs seeming to give out. "When?"

"Yesterday morning at the hotel," Aiden replied. "Someone apparently pushed him from the roof."

Victor removed his glasses, rubbing his eyes with shaking hands. "First Harrison, now Kevin." He looked up at them, suddenly suspicious. "Why are you telling me this? What do you think I know about it?"

"We're just trying to figure out what happened. We thought maybe you'd know something since Kevin visited you recently," Sam said.

"Yes," Victor confirmed, his voice steadier as he moved into his academic element. "He seemed particularly interested in the east wing Victorian features of the hotel."

"The finials?" Sam prompted.

Victor nodded, reaching for a stack of books. He pulled out a large historical architecture text, flipping it open to detailed drawings of Victorian rooflines. "These cast-iron decorative pieces crowned the east wing. They're valuable collector's items."

His hands moved with precision as he pointed to the illustrations, his academic expertise momentarily overriding his disheveled state. "The zinc-coated iron pieces develop a distinctive patina over time, you see. To collectors of architectural salvage, that patina is proof of authenticity. Each one is worth thousands to the right buyer. And, of course, it's easy to find the right buyer online these days."

"Did Kevin tell you why he was interested in them?" Aiden asked.

"He believed Harrison was removing the finials and other ironwork without proper authorization," Victor said. "He was comparing his recent insurance photos to some historical photos he'd seen at the bookstore. He'd discovered ornaments seemed to be missing."

Sam said, "Charlotte Webb showed me a book on the Ridgeview hotel."

Victor nodded. "Charlotte's always been interested in local history. Her family's been in Sunset Ridge for generations, so she knows all the old stories about the buildings and the people who worked in them." He hesitated. "Kevin asked if I'd help him build a case against Harrison. I said I would, but he never followed up. Of course, things have gotten so out of hand here that I don't know how much time I'd have had to help him." He gestured vaguely at the chaos around him.

"You're distracted with everything else going on," Sam said. Her gaze drifted to a gambling slip that had fallen from an overflowing desk drawer.

Victor flushed, noticing where she was looking. "I've been dealing with some personal issues."

"Like gambling," Aiden said directly, his tone gentle but firm.

The academic's shoulders slumped. For a moment, he looked as if he might deny it, but then he sighed. "I suppose it's obvious."

"Did Harrison know about your gambling, Victor?" Aiden asked.

Victor's expression hardened. "He did. And he used it against me. He approached me at a town council meeting last month and pulled me aside. 'I know about your little hobby, Professor,'" he mimicked in a sneering tone. "'Wouldn't the university board be interested to hear how their architectural historian is gambling away his paycheck?'"

"He blackmailed you," Sam concluded.

"In a manner of speaking," Victor confirmed bitterly. "He wanted me to stop opposing his development plans. Actually, he wanted me to publicly support them." He laughed humorlessly. "Can you imagine? Me, endorsing the destruction of buildings I've spent my career protecting?"

"You refused," Aiden guessed.

"Of course I refused!" Victor's voice rose before he caught himself. "Sorry. But yes, I told him to do his worst."

"And he did," Sam said quietly.

Victor nodded, the anger draining from him. "Harrison somehow found out about my online gambling debts. Maybe he saw my credit card statements when I left them on my desk, or overheard me on a phone call with creditors." His expression turned bitter. "Harrison was the type to pay attention to other people's weaknesses. He gathered enough evidence to make the university question my judgment. I sold my house to cover debts," Victor confirmed, gesturing around the makeshift living space. "Most of my possessions too. The town council allowed me to stay here temporarily as a caretaker while I get back on my feet."

"So you had reason to hate Harrison," Aiden said.

Victor nodded. "I did. I won't deny it." He looked between them, his expression suddenly vulnerable. "But I didn't kill him. Or Kevin. I had absolutely no reason to hurt Kevin; he was trying to stop Harrison too, in his own way."

"Trevor Mills saw you at the hotel recently," Sam said. "He said you were standing in the rain, staring at the hotel. That it was late at night."

Victor's face flushed. "After Kevin told me about the missing finials, I went over to document what was left. I wanted to see for myself how many had disappeared."

"Late at night?" Aiden asked skeptically.

"After what you told me about Harrison's death and what I knew about the missing finials, I had to see it for myself. I went at night because I didn't want to interfere with any police investigation."

Sam noticed a muddy pair of boots tucked partially under a stack of books. The mud looked fresh, not dried from days ago.

"Were you out this morning?" she asked.

"I was here. Inside," he insisted, though his voice wavered slightly. Victor followed Sam's gaze to the boots, then back up to meet her eyes. "I went out briefly to check the roof damage. There's a leak in the east corner."

The three sat in silence for a moment. Rain pattered against the windows, a gentle counterpoint to the tension in the room.

"I think Kevin found evidence connecting the missing ornamental pieces to Harrison's death," Sam finally said. "And it got him killed."

Victor looked thoughtful. "Do you know how Harrison was murdered?"

Aiden said, "It's looking like blunt-force trauma. Possibly from one of those missing finials. The zinc oxidation would explain the unusual marks on him."

Victor looked genuinely stunned. He shook his head. "Those finials are fairly heavy. They could certainly be lethal if used as a weapon."

"Who might have known which ones were valuable?" Sam asked. "Who had the expertise to identify them and remove them safely?"

Victor rubbed his face. "Besides me? Trevor Mills did the last restoration work for the hotel, so he'd know how they were attached. Diane Foster had access permits for her bat monitoring—she's been all over that east wing. I don't know if either Trevor or Diane would realize the value of the finials, though."

"And Kevin was investigating all of this," Aiden concluded.

"He must have figured out who was stealing them," Victor said quietly. "Or at least gotten too close."

Chapter Seventeen

Their visit wrapped up shortly afterward. As Sam and Aiden walked back to the truck, Aiden waited until they were out of earshot before speaking. "Well, that was informative."

"More than he intended, I think," Sam agreed.

"Those muddy boots were recent, despite his initial claim he hadn't left the building."

"I feel like he's hiding something," Sam said, "but I'm not convinced it's murder."

"Me either," Aiden replied thoughtfully. "His gambling problem gives him motive for theft, maybe, but not necessarily murder. Although I know he was furious with Harrison."

"Victor would definitely know which elements were most valuable to collectors."

Sam's conversation with Aiden wrapped up as they reached their vehicles outside the old library.

Aiden checked his watch. "I better get back to the school and help out the volunteers."

Sam nodded. "I'll let you know if I learn anything new."

As she started her car, her phone suddenly vibrated with incoming messages. Cell service was making a patchy comeback. Sam scrolled through the notifications—three texts from Lisa about Franklin, two from Olivia asking about generator oil, and one from Ginny Wilson that made her smile:

SOS! Drowning in storm cleanup. Need dog therapy ASAP. Informal agility gang meetup at my place 3pm. Dogs going stir-crazy and need to RUN.

Sam glanced at her growing mental to-do list, then thought about Arlo, who had been nothing but patient through all the chaos. Maybe Ginny was right and they could both use a break. She wondered if Diane would be back at this one. And if Diane had any thoughts on Kevin's death.

When Sam pulled up to Ginny's fifteen minutes later with Arlo in tow, several members of the agility club had already arrived, their dogs playing in the cleared yard. Ginny had managed to create an oasis of normalcy amid the storm aftermath. The massive oak in the corner had protected much of the space from wind damage, and the southern exposure meant the ground was already beginning to dry.

"You made it!" Ginny called, her curls bouncing as she waved enthusiastically from across the yard. "I was afraid you'd be too busy with your HOA duties."

Sam unclipped Arlo's leash, and he bounded over to join the play group, his small body quivering with excitement. "Even HOA presidents need breaks now and then."

Ginny laughed as she watched Arlo join the other dogs. Sam said, "Hey, I meant to tell you. You remember Franklin? The boy who's come over to watch the club a few times?"

"Of course I do. He's a great kid."

Sam said, "He is. Franklin also created a makeshift agility course back behind the community center. You might want to check it out. It's pretty amazing, especially since he made it all by hand."

"That's so cool! I'll run over there with Ziggy later on."

More people came into the yard, and Ginny hurried off to greet them.

Lucy Parker walked up with two bottles of water, offering one to Sam. Her silvery-blonde pixie cut caught the afternoon light, and her sharp green eyes followed Arlo as he tried to herd a much larger golden retriever. "Ziggy's been driving me crazy cooped up at home. We both needed this."

Sam accepted the water gratefully. "When did they clear your street? I know a lot of neighborhoods are still blocked by debris."

"They haven't cleared it yet," Lucy said with a laugh, automatically checking her fitness watch. "I found a detour through the Westfield trail. We had to climb over three fallen trees, but Ziggy considered it bonus agility practice."

The two women watched their dogs play for a moment.

"I've actually been meaning to talk to you," Lucy said casually. "Ziggy and I have been taking these insanely long walks since the storm. With everyone stuck at home, he needs the exercise, and I've been mapping the safest routes through town."

"That sounds like exactly what Ziggy would need," Sam said, knowing the whippet's energy level.

"It's been interesting seeing which areas were hit hardest," Lucy continued, taking a sip of water. "I walk past the hotel most mornings. I was there yesterday morning."

Sam tried not to show her immediate interest too obviously. "You were near the hotel yesterday?"

Lucy nodded. "I know about Kevin. I saw his Pathfinder parked at the hotel when I was on my morning route. I noticed because there aren't all that many vehicles driving around yet." She pulled out her phone. "Look at this—I've been taking pictures of storm damage to share with our running group so they can know what areas to avoid."

She scrolled through several photos of blocked streets and downed trees before stopping on one that showed the hotel. Kevin's distinctive Pathfinder was visible in the corner of the frame.

"What really caught my attention, though, was this truck," Lucy continued, swiping to another photo. "It came speeding out of there a few minutes later, which seemed weird because most vehicles have been moving so slowly through all the debris."

Sam studied the blurry image of a dark truck partially visible behind some branches. "Did you recognize it?"

"No, but Ziggy sure reacted to it," Lucy said, affectionately ruffling her dog's ears as he trotted over.

"What time was this?" Sam asked.

"Not long before I heard about Kevin," Lucy replied. "I was almost home when emergency vehicles started heading that direction." Her expression grew troubled. "I didn't connect the dots until I overheard a neighbor talking about Kevin being found at the hotel. That's when I remembered seeing his car there and the truck leaving in such a hurry."

Someone else walked up, and the conversation shifted to storm cleanup efforts, the challenges of working remotely without reliable internet, and the latest neighborhood gossip. But Lucy still looked concerned.

Chapter Eighteen

After heading home, Sam took some time to clear storm debris in her yard. Arlo helped by chasing squirrels and snapping his small jaws at a few bumblebees.

Later in the day, Olivia stopped by briefly. She and Sam talked about how to help Mandy and Alfred with their home repairs. Sam decided to call a neighborhood meeting, but needed it to be minus Mandy and Alfred. Olivia offered to invite them to help with the food pantry at the community center the next afternoon.

Sam spent an hour walking through Maple Hills, slipping printed notes into the small receptacles under mailboxes. *Important neighborhood meeting tomorrow 2 PM at clubhouse. Topic: Alfred and Mandy's house repairs: community support project. Please keep confidential.* She'd added a personal note to each: *Alfred and Mandy have been invited to help Olivia at the community center tomorrow afternoon with the food pantry at that time.*

That night, Sam turned in early, hoping to get an early start the next day. Arlo, apparently as tired as she was, curled up in a ball next to her and was soon snoring.

Sam hadn't set an alarm the night before, thinking she would be sure to wake up early. She was startled to see daylight streaming through the window when she finally did open her eyes. Arlo gave a sleepy yawn beside her. "We really slept in, little man," said Sam. Arlo's expression seemed to agree with her, although he appeared to have absolutely no regrets.

Sam was eating her breakfast when she received a delayed text message from Lucy that seemed to have been sent the night before.

Sam, I've been thinking again about that truck I saw leaving the hotel. I should probably report it to the police, but I'm helping out a neighbor tomorrow.

Sam texted back, offering to go to the station for her, asking Lucy to send the photos so she could make sure Chief Hawkins got them. After a while, Lucy got the text message, sent the photos, and told Sam she could give a formal statement sometime later.

Now, as Sam approached the modest brick building that housed the Sunset Ridge Police Department, she felt a twinge of apprehension. Chief Hawkins already viewed her with suspicion after finding both bodies. Bringing more information might only increase his wariness.

Inside, the normally quiet station buzzed with activity. Uniformed officers moved purposefully between desks, some talking on radios while others pored over maps spread across tables.

Sam approached the front desk, where Officer Jenny Martinez was sorting through a stack of handwritten reports.

"Is Chief Hawkins available?" Sam asked. "I have some information about Kevin Zhang's death that Lucy Parker asked me to give him. She couldn't come herself because of a neighbor's needs."

Jenny looked up, recognition flickering in her tired eyes. "He's in his office. I'll let him know you're here." She tapped her radio and spoke quietly into it.

A moment later, Chief Hawkins appeared in the doorway of his office. His stocky form seemed more imposing despite the exhaustion evident on his face. Dark circles shadowed his eyes.

"Ms. Prescott," he said, his tone neutral but guarded. "Martinez says you have information."

"I do," Sam replied. "If you have a minute."

He gestured toward his office without comment, stepping aside to let her enter. The small room was cluttered with emergency response plans, coffee cups, and a half-eaten sandwich.

"I'll be brief," Sam said as the chief settled into his chair. "I know you're busy with the storm response."

"And two homicides," he added pointedly, leaning back and studying her face.

Sam nodded. "That's why I'm here. I spoke with someone who was near the hotel, not long before I found Kevin."

Chief Hawkins raised an eyebrow, his pen poised over his notepad. "And who would that be?"

"Lucy Parker," Sam said. "She walks her dog early in the morning and has been noting safe routes after the storm. She saw Kevin's Pathfinder at the hotel, but more importantly, she photographed a truck speeding away from there shortly before I arrived."

She pulled out her phone, showing him the image Lucy had sent her—a blurry dark truck partially obscured by branches, but clearly in a hurry based on the spray of water from a puddle it had hit.

Chief Hawkins took her phone, studying the image with narrowed eyes. "This isn't much to go on. I can't even make out the license plate."

"I know," Sam admitted. "But whoever was driving that truck left the scene shortly before I arrived and found Kevin. They might have seen something. Or been involved."

The chief handed back her phone. "I'll talk to Ms. Parker and get her statement directly." He made a note in his pad. "Any idea what time this was taken?"

Sam right-clicked on the photo to get the metadata and showed it to the chief.

Chief Hawkins nodded slowly. "Anything else you want to share?"

Sam hesitated, then decided to test the waters. "Have you found anything unusual at either scene? Something that connects the two deaths?"

The chief's expression hardened. "You know I can't share details of an active investigation, especially with someone who discovered both bodies."

"I understand," Sam said, keeping her voice neutral. "I'm just wanting to help. Kevin called me for a reason. He thought I could help with something he discovered. He didn't specify what he'd found, but he mentioned it related to Harrison's death."

Chief Hawkins studied her for a long moment, as if weighing how much to share. Finally, he sighed, rubbing his forehead where deep lines had formed. He leaned forward, his chair creaking under his weight. "Ms. Prescott, I'm going to be straight with you. Finding two murder victims in two days doesn't look good. You've admitted to problems with Harrison Blackwood. Plus, you were the last person Kevin Zhang contacted before his death."

"I was trying to help Kevin."

"Maybe so," the chief conceded. "But until we sort this out, I'd appreciate it if you'd steer clear of the investigation." He paused, then added in a slightly softer tone, "That said, I appreciate you bringing this truck photo to my attention."

Sam recognized the dismissal in his tone. "Of course."

As Sam turned to leave, she noticed a whiteboard behind the door with names written in the chief's blocky handwriting. She recognized them immediately—Harrison Blackwood, Kevin Zhang, Victor Reid, Charlotte Webb, Trevor Mills, and her own name, connected by lines and question marks.

Chief Hawkins cleared his throat, drawing her attention back. "I'd still like a formal statement from you about finding Kevin's body, when you have time. Officer Martinez can take it now if you're available."

"Of course," Sam agreed, knowing it would keep her in the chief's good graces to cooperate fully. Before leaving, she and Jenny Martinez sat down for a few minutes so that Martinez could take her statement.

At two o'clock, Sam headed to the Maple Hills clubhouse for the meeting she'd called to talk about Alfred and Mandy's house. Everybody was supposed to keep the meeting under their hats, which she fervently hoped they'd been able to do.

The clubhouse had never been so crowded. And somehow, word had seemed to reach beyond the neighborhood, as Sam recognized several people who didn't live in Maple Hills. Sam stood beside the whiteboard she'd repurposed from HOA meetings, now showing a detailed plan for "Operation Jones Home Rescue." Around her, neighbors sat with coffee cups and notepads.

"Thanks for coming on short notice," Sam began, looking around at the filled chairs. "I know everyone's dealing with their own storm recovery, but we have neighbors who need our help."

She gestured to the whiteboard where she'd written the basic facts. "Alfred and Mandy's roof took major damage during the hurricane. Insurance will cover the repairs, but they're facing an eight-thousand-dollar deductible that has to be paid upfront before work can begin."

Murmurs rippled through the room as people absorbed the number.

"Eight thousand?" Mrs. Chen asked. "That's enormous for them."

"Exactly," Sam confirmed. "And here's why this matters to all of us. For fifteen years, Alfred and Mandy have been saving every extra dollar for a scholarship fund. They were finally ready to award it next month. It was their dream to help a local student attend technical college."

Nora stood up, her voice carrying across the room. "If they use that money for their deductible, fifteen years of sacrifice disappears."

"That's not happening on our watch," Marvin from the hardware store declared. "Alfred taught me half of what I know about basic contracting. Never charged me a dime."

An older gentleman raised his hand. "What exactly are we proposing?"

"Simple," Sam replied. "We pool our resources to cover their insurance deductible. They keep their scholarship fund intact, their roof gets fixed, and their dream stays alive."

"How much would each household need to contribute?" Lucy asked, already pulling out her checkbook.

Sam had done the math. "If twenty families participate, it's about four hundred dollars each. More families means less per household."

Hands started going up around the room.

"Count us in for our share," the Hendersons said simultaneously.

"Same here," added Mrs. Patterson. "Mandy brought me soup every day when I had pneumonia last winter."

Trevor, who had been quietly listening from the back, stepped forward. "I'll handle the insurance coordination and make sure everything's filed properly and the work gets scheduled as soon as the deductible's paid."

Within twenty minutes, Sam had commitments from eighteen families. The remaining amount was quickly covered when Nora announced that several neighbors who couldn't attend had already given her checks.

"The beautiful thing," Trevor said, his voice thick with emotion, "is that Alfred and Mandy have been doing this kind of thing for others their whole lives. It's about time someone returned the favor."

"When do we tell them?" someone asked.

"Once we have the full amount collected," Sam replied. "And we present it as a community investment in their scholarship, not charity. We're ensuring their generosity can continue exactly as they planned."

After wrapping up the meeting, Sam finally headed home.

She walked in to find her house strangely quiet. Ever since the seniors had relocated to the community center yesterday, the house felt almost too spacious. She still occasionally found reminders of their stay—a Scrabble tile under the sofa, a forgotten romance novel on the side table.

"Arlo?" she called, setting her keys on the entryway table.

The patter of small paws answered as Arlo trotted in from the kitchen, tail wagging with excitement. He'd clearly been napping on his favorite spot by the back door where afternoon sun created a warm patch on the hardwood floor.

The house felt almost too quiet after days of constant activity. The refrigerator hummed steadily, powered by the generator that continued to run without complaint. Outside, the distant sound of chainsaws cutting through fallen trees provided a reminder that recovery efforts continued throughout the neighborhood.

Sam checked her watch. It was only 4:00 PM, and she somehow still had some energy left. She decided to drive to the environmental monitoring station Diane had mentioned during their conversation at Ginny's. And Diane had invited her to come, after all.

Finding the converted carriage house wasn't difficult; it sat nestled among oak trees at the edge of town, its Victorian charm preserved despite the scientific equipment visible through the windows.

Sam hesitated before knocking. Her conversation with Chief Hawkins had made it clear she wasn't supposed to be investigating. But here she was, about to question another person connected to Harrison and Kevin. After all, though, the police were still waiting on the arrival of the state police and were also trying to help with storm recovery. Maybe she could help them get to the bottom of it.

When she finally knocked, Diane answered with a clipboard in her hand. Her dark hair was pulled back in a practical braid, and her hiking boots were caked with mud from early morning fieldwork.

"Sam, this is a surprise," Diane said, stepping back to let her in. Echo, the corgi, trotted forward to greet Sam with a welcoming bark and then a happy doggy grin.

"I hope I'm not interrupting," Sam replied, bending to give Echo a rub. "I decided to take you up on your invitation that you gave me at Ginny's. I'd have called ahead except . . . well, you know."

"The phones are still mainly down. Although I was able to get a text or two this morning. Come on inside."

Chapter Nineteen

Sam glanced around the station, genuinely impressed by the scientific setup. The space was filled with monitoring devices, sound recorders, and data collection tools organized with scientific precision. Colorful maps showing migration patterns and species distribution covered one wall.

"This is quite an operation you have here," Sam said.

Diane smiled, brightening at Sam's interest. "Environmental monitoring requires a lot of precision. I converted this old carriage house last year."

Echo circled Sam's legs, then settled at her feet with a contented sigh.

"It looks like you've got a good helper here, too."

Diane smiled fondly at the corgi. "He's the best. His job is morale booster."

I've actually been curious about something," Sam said, deciding on a forthright approach. "When we talked at Ginny's, you mentioned monitoring the hotel's bat habitats and that bats were in the hotel attic. Are they also roosting in some of the decorative features on the roof? Like the finials?"

Diane's eyes lit up. "Those decorative features are crucial, actually." She picked up a folder of photographs. "Especially in historic buildings like the Ridgeview."

Sam moved closer to look at the images. "In what way?"

"See these ornamental features?" Diane pointed to a close-up of a finial. "Their design creates perfect roosting spots for the bats."

Sam studied the photograph, noticing the small creatures nestled in the curved elements. "I never would have thought of that."

"Most people don't." Diane turned to another image. "These leaf patterns and hollow sections provide ideal sheltered spaces. Each finial supported part of the colony."

"And removing the finials would disrupt the habitat," Sam concluded.

"Exactly." Diane nodded, her professional demeanor briefly overtaken by genuine enthusiasm. "That's one reason I was so opposed to Harrison's renovation plans. And why I'm now concerned about the missing finials."

"Missing?" Sam tried to sound as if she didn't know about them.

Diane nodded. "I went to the hotel after the storm to see how the building had held up. That's when I noticed that several of the finials had disappeared. At first I thought it might have been storm damage, but when I climbed the scaffolding, I saw they were removed too cleanly for that. It's a pity. The bats have been displaced from their roosting spot, although they're still in the attic."

Sam shifted the subject. "The hotel seems to have become something of an inhospitable place. I suppose you heard about Kevin."

Diane nodded again. "Yes. I was sorry to hear that. It was a while before I got the news, with cell service being mostly down. And, of course, I was out of pocket that morning, anyway, conducting field surveys over at the wetlands on the north side of town." Diane spread her documentation on a table, including a field notebook with detailed timestamps. "I was gone from dawn until about nine, checking storm damage to the habitat there. Solo, as usual."

"I see," Sam said. It almost sounded as if Diane had delivered this little speech before, perhaps to the police. It didn't really constitute an alibi, since Diane had been out there solo. "It's good you're assessing the storm's environmental impact," Sam said. "I'm sure it was disruptive for wildlife."

"That's why I maintain meticulous records," Diane replied, tapping her notebook. "Scientific accuracy matters."

Echo, who had been quiet, suddenly stood and whined softly.

"Easy, Echo," Diane murmured, stroking the corgi's head. "He's been unsettled since the storm."

"I guess animals pick up on our stress too," Sam observed.

"That's true. Echo's been my research companion for years. He's more sensitive than most scientific instruments."

"Going back to Kevin, did you know him well?" Sam asked, changing tack.

"Barely," Diane said, flipping past several photos quickly. "We spoke briefly about the environmental impact report Harrison was trying to alter, but that's all."

"The last time we talked, you mentioned that Harrison's plans were also going to affect your dad's nature center."

Diane hesitated, then sighed. "My father's nature center would have lost its parking access under Harrison's plans." Her voice softened. "The center is his life's work—everything he built after my mother died. Harrison knew it would essentially shut us down if visitors couldn't park."

"That sounds deliberate," Sam said.

"It was." Diane pulled out a copy of an environmental impact study with sections clearly edited. "Look at these pages. He had someone remove all mention of the protected bat species before submitting it to the town council."

Sam examined the document, noting the obvious discrepancies between drafts. "That seems illegal."

"It absolutely was."

"You must have been furious," Sam said, watching Diane's reaction carefully.

Diane's eyes met Sam's, and something shifted in her expression. "I wasn't the only one Harrison had crossed," she said, her tone changing as she seemed to realize what Sam might be implying. "I didn't have anything to do with his death."

"I'm just trying to understand what happened," Sam responded, keeping her tone neutral.

Diane shook her head, a small smile playing on her lips. "I suppose that's natural, given you found both bodies. But if you're looking into possible motives, you should know I wasn't alone in opposing Harrison's plans."

She gestured toward her research materials. "Charlotte Webb was fighting just as hard to stop his downtown development. Her bookstore was directly threatened." She paused. "And if you're thinking about people with detailed knowledge of the hotel's architecture, Charlotte knows the hotel's history well."

Sam noticed how Diane seemed more relaxed now that the conversation had shifted away from her own conflicts with Harrison. "Her great-aunt worked there for decades. And you should probably talk to Victor Reid and Trevor Mills. They both know that building inside and out."

"I'll be sure to do that. Thanks, Diane. I won't keep you any longer. And thanks for taking the time to explain your work."

"Anytime," Diane replied.

As Sam left, she noticed the roads were clearer that evening, with crews making steady progress removing fallen trees and repairing power lines. She spotted families working together in yards, piling debris at curbs and patching damaged roofs.

By the time she reached home, the shadows were lengthening. She was checking the generator oil levels when her phone chimed with a text message. She smiled when she saw Aiden's name on the screen. *Made pasta sauce from rapidly defrosting ingredients. Too much for one person. My place at 6:30? We can compare notes on the case.*

She hesitated, her finger hovering over the screen. There was something undeniably personal about visiting Aiden's home. It felt like crossing a threshold.

"What do you think, buddy? A professional discussion over pasta, is all it is," she said, as much to convince herself as Arlo. She was far from being a professional investigator, and Aiden had left the police force for teaching. But if it wasn't professional, what was it?

The little dog tilted his head doubtfully, his expressive eyes seeming to see right through her pretense.

After Chad, she'd made a rule about relationships—don't. The divorce had taught her that even careful people could miss obvious red flags. She wasn't ready to test her judgment again.

And yet, Aiden wasn't Chad. She'd seen how he interacted with others in the community, how he stepped up without needing recognition, how he respected her own leadership while offering support. There was a steadiness to him that Chad had never possessed.

Her phone chimed again: *You can bring Arlo if you'd like. I've got those biscuits he likes.*

A smile tugged at her lips despite her reservations. The fact that he'd remembered Arlo's favorite treats was just another small example of how he paid attention to details that mattered.

"He's got your number," she told Arlo, who perked up at her changed tone.

She picked up her phone, typing a quick reply before she could overthink it: *Thanks! We'll be there in a minute.*

As soon as she hit send, a flutter of nerves swept through her stomach. It was just dinner to discuss the case, she reminded herself. Not a date.

"Come on, Arlo," she said, clipping on his leash. "Let's go see what Aiden's cooked up. But remember," she pointed a finger at her dog, who wagged his tail innocently, "we're just there to work on the case. Nothing more."

Arlo gave a small bark that sounded suspiciously like disagreement.

"Traitor," she said affectionately, locking the door behind them.

The sun hung low over the mountains as Sam headed over to Aiden's. He lived in a modest craftsman bungalow built in the 1930s that predated the subdivision. Even in the waning daylight, she could see the distinctive character of the home with its low-pitched roof and wide front porch. A massive oak tree in the front yard had dropped several branches during the storm, but they'd been neatly stacked at the curb. The house itself appeared to have suffered minimal damage, though a blue tarp covered one corner of the roof.

Sam and Arlo walked down the driveway. She'd been reluctant to accept his invitation initially, sensing that visiting his home crossed some invisible line in their undefined relationship. But the practicality of comparing notes on the investigation had overridden her hesitation.

Arlo grinned as he trotted toward Aiden's front door. "Be on your best behavior," she told him, though the little dog had never been anything but charming to everyone he met.

Aiden opened the door before she reached the porch, his tall frame filling the doorway. The familiar sight of him, now in a faded flannel shirt and jeans rather than his emergency coordination clothes, sent that small flutter through her chest that she was becoming accustomed to ignoring.

"Glad you could come," said Aiden with a warm smile. "Both of you."

Chapter Twenty

"Oh, it's our pleasure," Sam replied, trying not to look too obvious as she took in his living space. The interior surprised her with its orderliness, not at all what she expected from a bachelor's home. "Your place survived the storm pretty well."

"I lost a few shingles and one window, but it's nothing compared to what others are dealing with," Aiden said, closing the door behind them.

He bent down to greet Arlo, who was straining against his leash for attention. "Hey there, buddy. I've got something for you." From his pocket, he produced a small dog biscuit, earning him immediate adoration from Arlo.

"Wow, you're prepared," said Sam, smiling.

"I've got my former detective training to thank for that," Aiden replied with a grin. "I'm always gathering information. I noticed the brand in your pantry when I stopped by your house last time."

The thoughtfulness of that small detail caught Sam off guard. Chad had never paid attention to such things.

"I can give you the nickel tour," Aiden offered, leading them through the living room.

The space was simply furnished but comfortable, with a leather sofa and coffee table, a well-worn reading chair, and bookshelves built into the walls. They were filled with a mixture of local history volumes, teaching materials, and crime novels. A collection of black and white photographs of Sunset Ridge's historic buildings lined one wall, including several of the Ridgeview House hotel in its heyday.

"Did you take these pictures?" Sam asked, stopping to examine a striking image of the fountain downtown.

"Yeah, photography kind of became my thing when I was on the force," Aiden explained. "It helped me notice details. And it was a way to relax after a rough day on the job."

The kitchen was a warm space with original cabinetry painted a soft blue and updated with modern countertops. A round oak table sat in an adjacent breakfast nook surrounded by windows. The table was already set for two, with case files and photographs neatly arranged at one end.

"This is really nice," Sam said, genuinely impressed by the character of the home and how well it suited him.

"Thanks. The house needed work when I bought it, but the bones were good," Aiden replied.

He gestured toward the table. "I made a basic pasta. Nothing fancy, but I thought we could eat while we go through everything."

"That sounds perfect. It smells amazing," Sam said, unclipping Arlo's leash. The little dog immediately began a thorough exploration of his new surroundings.

Aiden served the pasta, a simple dish with cherry tomatoes, herbs, and parmesan.

"This looks amazing," said Sam. She realized she hadn't eaten much at all that day.

He smiled at her. "Well, it's sustenance, anyway. How did your day go today?"

"I did pick up some information I wanted to share with you. Ginny had the agility club over at her house yesterday to let the dogs run around. Lucy was there with Ziggy and showed me a picture of a truck that had been leaving the hotel around the time Kevin was killed."

Aiden raised his eyebrows. "How clear was the photo?"

"Unfortunately, not very. It was pretty blurry. She couldn't get to the police this morning, so I took it to Hawkins."

Aiden said, "That's still useful information. It could have been the perpetrator or someone who saw something."

"They were driving fast, according to Lucy. She thought that was unusual because everybody has been taking it easy on the roads with all the debris. So maybe it was actually the murderer."

Aiden's kitchen timer interrupted them, and he rose to retrieve a loaf of garlic bread from the oven. The domestic normality of the moment struck Sam as surreal given the gravity of their conversation.

"So, let's run through our suspects again," Aiden said, returning to the table. "Victor Reid knows the architecture inside out, has money troubles, and despised Harrison. Plus he was pretty evasive about where he was, and those muddy boots seemed pretty fresh for someone who claims he's been holed up in the library."

"Trevor also placed him at the hotel recently and thought Victor is behaving erratically. Then there's Charlotte Webb with her extensive knowledge of the building's history," Sam continued. "She fought Harrison over her bookstore, and somebody saw them arguing shortly before his death."

"Trevor Mills lost that big contract to Harrison, definitely has the skills to remove those finials, and Victor mentioned seeing him poking around the hotel recently. Although Trevor has more right to be there than Victor does."

"Right. And Diane Foster had those special access permits for her bat monitoring," Sam finished. "She was fighting Harrison over environmental protections, and she's been all over that east wing where Harrison was found. I spoke with her today, and she has no alibi for Kevin's death."

They fell into a comfortable rhythm, discussing each suspect's motives, means, and opportunities. Sam found herself relaxing as they worked through the evidence, appreciating how easily they complemented each other's thinking.

"You know who keeps sticking in my mind? Diane," Aiden said after they'd cleared their plates. "Think about it—her environmental permit gave her access to pretty much anywhere in the hotel, including after hours when nobody's around to ask questions."

"And she could easily document all those structural elements without raising any red flags," Sam pointed out. "Everyone would just assume she's monitoring her bats."

"Exactly. And we know she's not afraid to go to extremes for causes she believes in," Aiden said. "I looked up that case she won in D.C.—she actually infiltrated a construction company to gather evidence of environmental violations. That takes serious determination."

A knock at the door interrupted them, and Arlo dashed toward the sound with a welcoming bark.

"That's probably Olivia," Aiden said, rising from his chair. "She mentioned stopping by with updates."

When Aiden opened the door, Olivia stood on the porch with a large insulated bag. Her auburn hair was pulled back in a practical ponytail, though wisps had escaped around her face.

"Hope I'm not crashing the party," she said with a small smile, glancing between them. "Just finished at the community center and thought you two might appreciate some chocolate cake. Mike from the barbecue place brought it for the volunteers."

"Not at all," Sam assured her. "Come on in. We were just going through the case."

"Are you making any progress?" Olivia asked, setting the bag on the counter and kneeling to greet Arlo, who was beside himself with excitement at her arrival.

"We were just comparing notes on our suspects," Aiden explained, bringing plates for the cake.

"The whole town's going to breathe easier when this is figured out," Olivia said, unpacking the dessert. "All the talk at the food bank today has been about the murders. People are pretty on edge, especially with emergency services already stretched so thin."

"How's everything going with the distribution?" Sam asked, accepting a slice of the rich chocolate cake.

"Better than I expected, actually. We've got a good system going now. Jason's been amazing at finding ways around all the blocked roads." Olivia helped herself to a small piece of cake and leaned against the counter. "Oh, I saw Diane Foster at Charlotte's bookstore today having what looked like a pretty intense conversation."

Sam looked up with interest. "Diane and Charlotte? Could you tell what they were talking about?"

"I couldn't hear all of it, but they were in the back room when I arrived to drop off meals. Charlotte seemed really upset about something. She said something like, 'We can't wait any longer. Kevin probably figured it out. Maybe he even mentioned it to others.' When they saw me, they immediately stopped talking." Olivia lowered her voice.

"Did they explain what they were discussing?" Aiden asked, keeping his tone casual.

"No. They were eager to change the subject. When I asked if they needed help with anything, they both seemed really anxious for me to leave." Olivia took another bite of cake. "The weird part was that I overheard Diane say something about 'midnight at the old library' as I was leaving."

"That's kind of weird," Aiden said. "When was this?"

"Early afternoon. I've been taking meals to businesses that are trying to reopen." Olivia glanced between them. "Is that helpful at all?"

"Everything helps," Sam said. "Now it's just a matter of trying to piece it all together."

Olivia nodded, then checked her watch. "I should probably get back. We're setting up temporary housing in the high school gym for families who can't stay in their homes."

After Olivia left with promises to keep them updated, Sam and Aiden returned to the table, the atmosphere noticeably shifted.

"So Diane and Charlotte are planning something," Sam said slowly. "And they mentioned Kevin figuring it out."

"It could be completely innocent, of course. Maybe they're talking about helping Victor rescue the old library from development."

"True," Sam agreed. "But why the secrecy? And why mention Kevin?"

"The timing is weird, for sure," Aiden said. "Could all three of them have been in on Harrison's death somehow? And then Kevin found out?"

As they continued reviewing their notes, Sam found herself increasingly aware of Aiden's presence across the table. Their hands brushed accidentally as they reached for the same photograph, sending that now-familiar jolt through her fingertips.

"Sorry," they said simultaneously, then laughed at the synchronicity.

The moment stretched between them, comfortable and charged at the same time. For a brief second, Sam allowed herself to imagine what it might be like to let her guard down completely with this man.

The sharp ring of Sam's phone broke the spell. It had been so long since a phone call had made it through that she jumped. Sam glanced at the screen, surprised to see Lucy Parker's name.

"Lucy? Is everything okay?" Sam asked.

Chapter Twenty-One

"Sam, I'm at the downtown construction site that's not far from the hotel," Lucy's voice came through breathlessly. "I was walking Ziggy on our usual route when I noticed something strange in the debris. It's this large metal piece. It looks like it might have come from the hotel's roof. It's got this really distinctive pattern on it, almost like leaves or vines."

Sam's eyes widened as she looked at Aiden. They both recognized the description immediately.

"That sure sounds like it," Sam said, trying to keep her voice calm.

"It's about two feet tall, looks like cast iron, pretty heavy. It was partially buried under some construction materials, but Ziggy kept pulling toward it. And Sam, there's something else. There's a bag here with what looks like a camera and notebook in it. The bag has Kevin's initials on it."

"Be sure not to touch anything. Have you called the police?"

"I just did. Chief Hawkins said he's sending Officer Martinez, but it might take her a while to get here with all the road closures and from where she is. I thought you might want to know right away. I know you've been looking into this stuff."

"I'm on my way with Aiden," Sam said, already standing. "Stay there, but keep your distance from everything, okay?"

After hanging up, Sam and Aiden exchanged a look of excitement mixed with apprehension.

"Maybe Lucy just found the murder weapon," said Aiden.

"And Kevin's camera might have proof of who took it."

As they headed for the door, Arlo trailing at their heels, Sam glanced back at Aiden's kitchen. The remains of their meal, the case files spread across the table, the feeling of comfortable partnership, all felt like a glimpse into a possibility she wasn't quite ready to acknowledge.

"Let's go see what Lucy found," she said.

Aiden nodded. "I'll come too, but I'll follow in my own car in case I get called away. Should we bring Arlo?"

Sam glanced at her dog, who had curled up contentedly on a rug after their meal. "Better not. If Lucy's found something connected to the case, we don't want Arlo potentially disturbing a crime scene. Let's drop him by my house on the way."

A few minutes later, Sam was unlocking her front door. The house felt eerily quiet after the constant activity of the past few days. She quickly refreshed Arlo's water bowl and set out a small treat.

"Sorry, buddy," she said, giving him a scratch behind the ears. "Duty calls. We won't be long."

Arlo seemed to understand, padding over to his fluffy bed and settling down with a contented sigh.

The streets were still littered with debris, but Sam could see signs of progress as she followed Aiden's truck toward the downtown area where Lucy was waiting.

When they pulled up near the partially cleared lot where Harrison had planned his controversial downtown development, Lucy was waiting beside her car. Her silvery-blonde pixie cut caught the afternoon sunlight as she waved them over.

"You made it," Lucy said, relief in her voice. "I wasn't sure if the roads would be passable near this section from your house."

"We had to take the long way around," Sam replied, stepping over a fallen branch. "What did you find?"

Lucy gestured toward the wooded area behind the development site. "I probably shouldn't have been poking around here, but Ziggy was acting weird this evening. He kept pulling me toward those trees back there, which he never does."

Lucy gestured toward the wooded area behind the development site. "It's over there, partially buried under some debris. The rain washed away enough soil that I could see something metallic underneath. I didn't want to disturb it, but you can see it clearly from here."

She led them to the spot, pointing carefully. "There—that ornate metal piece. And there's a bag right next to it."

Sam and Aiden exchanged glances before studying the partially buried evidence from a respectful distance. "That's a finial," Sam said, recognizing the distinctive leaf pattern even through the mud.

Sam studied the finial without touching it, noting the bluish-white edges of zinc oxidation Charlotte had described. Dark stains on some of the ornate leaf detailing made her stomach turn.

"Kevin must have discovered this was missing from the hotel. And who took it," said Sam quietly.

Lucy said, "Do you think this is why somebody killed him?"

They heard an engine approaching, and Sam tensed until she recognized Chief Hawkins's police SUV, followed by a county crime scene van.

"Ms. Parker," Chief Hawkins acknowledged as he stepped out, looking exhausted. His expression shifted when he spotted Sam and Aiden. "I should've known you two would be here already."

"Lucy called us," Sam explained simply.

"I thought Officer Martinez was coming," Lucy said.

The chief rubbed his forehead. "She's responding to a multi-car accident on Highway 9. I was already heading downtown, so I took the call." He gestured to the technicians unloading equipment. "Would you mind showing us exactly where you found these items?"

As Lucy walked the technicians to the wooded area, Chief Hawkins turned to Sam and Aiden.

"I appreciate your interest in this case, but this is a double homicide investigation. I can't have civilians contaminating my crime scenes."

"We understand completely," Aiden replied. "We're only here because Lucy called."

"What brought you here in the first place?" the chief asked Lucy as she rejoined them.

"I walk through here with Ziggy," she explained. "I've been mapping safe routes since the storm for folks in my neighborhood. Ziggy started acting strangely, pulling me toward those trees." She nodded toward the wooded area.

Chief Hawkins made notes on his small pad. "And the truck you mentioned seeing earlier? I don't think we've gotten your statement yet."

"It was a dark pickup, moving much too fast considering all the debris on the roads," Lucy confirmed. "I couldn't make out the driver or license plate."

A technician approached, holding up the evidence-bagged camera. "Chief? We've got an intact memory card here."

Chief Hawkins followed the technician back to the van. Sam watched, wishing she could see what Kevin had documented.

"I should get going," Lucy said, checking her watch. "My sister is dropping off my niece for the evening so she and her husband can get some work done around the house."

"Thank you for calling us," Sam said, giving her friend's arm a gentle squeeze. "Your observation skills might have just broken this case wide open."

"More like Ziggy's skills. I hope they catch whoever did this."

After Lucy left with Ziggy, Sam turned to Aiden. "Do you think the chief will share anything about what's on that camera?"

"Not likely," Aiden replied.

Chief Hawkins returned, studying Sam with an unreadable expression before seeming to come to a decision.

"I've been hard on you two, especially you, Sam," he finally said. "But evidence is suggesting you stumbled into this situation rather than caused it."

Sam was surprised by the admission. "I just want to help find whoever is responsible."

The chief nodded. "Kevin's camera footage contains extensive documentation of the hotel's roofline, particularly the east wing. We understand some of the ornaments have been disappearing."

"Like the finial," Sam said.

"Exactly." Chief Hawkins lowered his voice. "The lab will confirm, but it appears this finial matches the wound pattern on Harrison Blackwood. Evidence suggests it was deliberately removed from the hotel before the storm hit."

Sam processed this information. "Why would someone hide it here instead of disposing of it completely?"

"That's what we need to determine," the chief said. "Bringing evidence here was a risk. But maybe the perpetrator ran out of time."

An officer interrupted with a radio message. "County investigators need you back at the station, Chief. The state forensics team just arrived."

Chief Hawkins nodded, turning back to Sam and Aiden. "I need to go. Despite what I've shared, I need you two to step back from this investigation. This killer has already claimed two victims." He handed Sam his card. "If you find anything else, call me directly. Don't attempt to handle it yourselves."

After the chief left, Sam and Aiden watched the crime scene team working methodically through the wooded area.

"We should leave," Aiden finally said. "There's nothing more we can learn here now."

As they walked back to their vehicles, Sam's thoughts raced. "After what Olivia told us about Charlotte and Diane's private conversation, I should talk to Charlotte. But it's getting late now. Maybe I should tackle it tomorrow."

"Not a bad idea. You've had a full day. And I doubt Charlotte is at the bookshop at this point." Aiden gave her a smile. "I'll check in on you tomorrow. Sweet dreams."

Chapter Twenty-Two

Sam started to head home, but the thought of being alone with her thoughts suddenly didn't feel appealing. Without consciously planning it, she drove toward the Smiths' modest ranch house in Maple Hills.

Lisa answered the door, her nurse's scrubs suggesting she'd just returned from a shift at the hospital. Her exhausted smile brightened when she saw Sam.

"This is perfect timing," Lisa said. "Franklin's been asking when he could show you the improvements to his agility course. He's been sketching designs all morning."

"I could use a break from everything," Sam admitted. "Is he up for a short field trip before the sun goes down?"

Lisa called over her shoulder, "Franklin! Sam's here to see your agility course."

The sound of rapid footsteps preceded Franklin's appearance, his face lighting up when he saw Sam. He clutched a spiral notebook with colored tabs sticking out from various pages.

"You came!" he said, grinning at her. "I've added three new obstacles since you found me there."

"That sounds impressive," Sam replied. "Should we bring Arlo and check it out? Before the sun goes down?"

Franklin nodded enthusiastically. "Mom, can I go with Sam to the community center? Please?"

"Of course," Lisa said. "Just be home before dinner. And remember what we talked about regarding the community center property."

Franklin nodded solemnly. "I know. It's public land, and my course is just temporary until the real agility field is fixed."

Ten minutes later, Sam pulled into the community center parking lot with Franklin and Arlo in tow, after she'd run by the house to grab the little dog. As they walked toward the baseball field, Franklin explained his latest improvements with the precision of an engineer three times his age.

"I measured the distances between obstacles using a tape measure I borrowed from Mr. Jones," he explained, flipping open his notebook to show Sam a diagram that could have been created by a professional course designer. "The specifications say eighteen feet is optimal for dogs Arlo's size."

"You've been doing your research."

"I like when things are exactly right," Franklin replied. "Some kids think it's weird that I care about measurements so much."

"Being precise isn't weird," Sam assured him. "It's actually really useful."

Franklin's expression brightened. "That's what I tried to tell my friend Jake. He said I should just throw a course together without measuring anything. But then how would I know if it's safe?"

Sam bit back a smile at his indignation. "Not everyone appreciates the value of proper planning. You're just ahead of the game."

What had been an impressive makeshift setup had been refined with a few thoughtful touches. Franklin had added small handwritten signs identifying each element and repositioned obstacles for better spacing.

"You've been busy," Sam remarked, taking in the meticulous improvements.

"The Parks and Recreation supervisor came by yesterday," Franklin explained. "I thought he was going to make me take it down, but he actually liked it. He said as long as I don't damage anything and keep it safe, the course can stay until the regular agility field is repaired."

"Hey, that's great news!"

"He even helped me put up this," Franklin added proudly, pointing to a small bulletin board attached to a tree. A laminated sign read "Temporary Agility Course" with a neatly printed schedule below it. "Now people can sign up for practice times so it doesn't get too crowded."

"You've thought of everything," Sam said, noting the careful organization of the signup sheet, complete with time slots and spaces for owner and dog names.

Franklin shrugged, though his pleased expression belied his casual response. "I just like it when stuff makes sense."

Arlo waited impatiently at the starting line, clearly eager to begin his run. Sam took him through the warm-up routine while Franklin pulled out his stopwatch.

For the next forty-five minutes, Sam lost herself in the simple joy of working with Arlo on the course. Franklin proved to be an attentive observer, suggesting minor adjustments that showed a lot of insight for someone his age. The concerns of the investigation temporarily receded as Sam focused on Arlo's enthusiastic runs and Franklin's earnest coaching.

They took a break on a fallen log that Franklin had repurposed as a bench. Sam noticed several adults with dogs on the far side of the clearing, watching with interest.

"Miss Ginny from the agility club came by yesterday," Franklin told her, following her gaze. "She said my course design was 'innovative' and took pictures to show the club."

"That doesn't surprise me at all," Sam replied. "You have a real talent for this."

"Do you think . . . " Franklin hesitated, suddenly shy. "Do you think when they rebuild the real course, they might let me help design parts of it?"

"I think that's a great idea," Sam said. "The club would be lucky to have your input."

Franklin beamed, then grew serious. "I was worried they'd think I'm just a kid, or that I shouldn't be involved because I don't even have my own dog."

"Good ideas can come from anybody," Sam assured him. "And you've obviously proven your skills with this course."

"Mom says I shouldn't get too attached to the idea," Franklin added, his expression clouding slightly. "She says sometimes adults have their own ideas about how things should be done."

"That's sometimes true," Sam acknowledged. "But in this case, you've already impressed the right people. Ginny has considerable influence in the agility club."

As Arlo completed another run, this time with Franklin handling him while Sam observed, Sam noticed the little dog seemed more relaxed than he had been in days. The simple rhythm of the course, the clear expectations, and the predictable pattern all provided comfort amid the chaos.

"He really loves this, doesn't he?" Franklin said, watching Arlo prance back with obvious pride.

"He does," Sam agreed. "We all need routines, especially during tough times."

Sam watched as Franklin meticulously repositioned the obstacles. "You've got a real eye for detail. I was the same way at your age."

"Really?" Franklin looked up, genuinely interested.

"My parents weren't exactly the organized type," Sam said, choosing her words carefully. "I guess I started making lists and planning things because someone had to." She smiled, pushing away the memory of missed school conferences and empty refrigerators. "It became my superpower."

Franklin nodded seriously. "Like how I keep track of things for my mom when she's working extra shifts. She forgets stuff sometimes since the divorce."

"That's not easy," she said gently. "How long ago did they divorce?"

"Eight months and seventeen days," Franklin replied without hesitation. "Mom says we're adjusting well, but she still cries sometimes when she thinks I'm asleep."

His matter-of-fact tone couldn't quite hide the concern beneath it. Sam recognized the weight of responsibility in his young eyes, a child trying to manage an adult's pain.

"I know what that's like," Sam said. "After my divorce, I thought I had to keep everything perfect, as if organizing my kitchen cabinets would somehow fix what was broken."

Franklin's eyes widened slightly. "You're divorced too? Like my parents?"

"I am," Sam confirmed. "It's been a little while now."

"Does it get easier?" he asked, his voice smaller suddenly.

Sam considered her answer carefully. "Yes, it does. Not right away, and not all at once, but gradually. Your mom will cry less, and you'll both find your new normal."

Franklin made one final adjustment to the hurdle, then stood back to survey his work. "Perfect," he declared, then glanced at Sam. "Did your parents think it was weird? That you were so organized?"

The question caught her off guard. "They didn't really notice," she admitted. "They were distracted by other things." Or, if they did notice, they weren't impressed.

"My dad used to say I was too fussy about stuff," Franklin said, adjusting the measuring tape in his hands. "Mom says it's just how my brain works, but Dad thought I should be playing sports instead of measuring things."

"Some people don't understand that having things in order helps us make sense of the world," Sam said. "It took me a long time to realize that being organized wasn't something to be embarrassed about. It's definitely a strength."

"My mom gets it," Franklin said. "She says I'm her little assistant manager. I help her remember bill days and when to buy groceries. Dad used to handle all that stuff."

"Smart woman, your mom."

Franklin beamed, then his expression grew more serious. "Do you still see your parents? You never talk about them."

Sam hesitated. She rarely discussed her family situation, preferring to keep that part of her life firmly in the past. But Franklin's open face and the honesty of his question deserved the same in return.

"Not really," she said finally. "We don't have much in common. After I sold my app and had some success, they wanted to be involved in my life again, but only because of what I could give them, not because they wanted to know me." She hadn't meant to say so much, but there was something about Franklin's quiet attentiveness that made it easy to be honest.

"That stinks," Franklin said, with the straightforward clarity of the young.

Sam laughed softly. "Yes. It does. But you know what? It taught me that you can build your own family. Look around," she gestured to the neighborhood beyond the trees. "All these people coming together after the storm, helping each other. That's a kind of family too."

Franklin considered this, then nodded.

Chapter Twenty-Three

The next morning, Sam decided to stop by Charlotte's bookstore before the day got too hectic.

Main Street showed more signs of recovery in the early morning light. Several shops had reopened, their windows no longer boarded up. Work crews were making steady progress clearing debris, and the community was clearly rallying despite everything.

Sam's stomach reminded her she'd skipped breakfast in her eagerness to get downtown. She made a mental note to grab something from the bakery after talking with Charlotte, assuming the bookstore was open this early.

To her relief, the open sign hung in the window of Twice-Told Tales. Through the window, she could see Charlotte already at work, organizing books.

Sam parked quickly and hurried to the door. The familiar bell jingled as she pushed open the door, and the comforting scent of old books greeted her.

"Charlotte?" she called, stepping inside.

Charlotte looked up from a stack of books she was arranging on a newly dried shelf. Her dark brown hair had escaped its usual messy bun in several places.

"What a nice surprise." Charlotte set down her book and moved toward the counter. She gestured around at the significantly improved store interior. "What do you think? The dehumidifiers have been running non-stop."

Sam took in the transformation. The mud line on the walls remained visible, but the floors were dry, and most of the inventory had been salvaged and reorganized.

"It looks amazing, Charlotte. You've made incredible progress since day-before-yesterday."

Charlotte smiled, though the exhaustion was evident in her eyes. "Yesterday, I had students from the high school again. They showed up with cleaning supplies and spent most of the day here. I fed them whatever snacks I could scrounge up."

She flipped off the small desk lamp to conserve battery power. "What brings you by? I heard about Kevin Zhang. Terrible news, coming so soon after Harrison."

Sam nodded, choosing her approach carefully. "It's actually Kevin's death that's brought me here. With everything that's happened, I'm trying to make sense of it all."

"Of course." Charlotte gestured toward two chairs in the reading nook. "Though I'm not sure how much help I'll be with everything still so chaotic around town."

As they sat, Sam noticed a stack of papers beside Charlotte's chair—detailed maps of what looked like the old library building with certain areas circled in red. Charlotte discreetly slid a book over them when she noticed Sam's glance.

"Just some storm damage assessment," she explained with a small smile.

Sam nodded, deciding on a gentle approach. "I heard there might be something happening at the old library tonight. I was concerned, with everything going on around town."

Charlotte's expression flickered briefly before settling into something more composed. "Oh? Where did you hear that?"

"Around town," Sam replied vaguely, not wanting to implicate Olivia. "With two deaths so close together, people are understandably on edge."

A moment of silence stretched between them before Charlotte sighed, removing her glasses to clean them with the edge of her cardigan.

"It's not what you might think," she said quietly. "Diane and I are relocating the endangered bats from the hotel. The storm damaged their habitat in the east wing, and with all the renovation uncertainty now that Harrison's gone, they need a safe space."

"And that place is the old library?" Sam asked, relief evident in her voice.

Charlotte nodded. "It has similar architectural features—hollow cornices, protected spaces in the attic. Victor agreed to let us relocate the colony there temporarily."

"Why the secrecy?"

"It's not exactly by the book." Charlotte looked uncomfortable. "Diane has permits for monitoring the bats, not relocating them. But with the hotel's future uncertain, she couldn't risk losing the entire colony. And, obviously, the town doesn't know about us putting bats in the old library. Diane thought it might be better to ask forgiveness than ask permission."

Sam nodded, understanding now. "That totally makes sense. I'm glad it's nothing more serious."

"Did you think it was connected to the murders?" Charlotte asked.

"Kevin was investigating something about the hotel before he died. I wondered if it might be related."

"There was something Kevin mentioned that seemed odd," Charlotte said. "I don't think I mentioned it to you. He said he'd seen someone on the hotel scaffolding after hours before the storm. He couldn't tell who it was in the dark."

"Did he report it?" Sam asked.

"He was planning to, but then the storm hit." Charlotte's expression grew troubled. "He seemed to think whoever it was knew exactly what they were doing. They moved around that scaffolding like they'd been up there before."

Sam nodded, absorbing this information. "It sure sounds suspicious."

The bell on the door rang, and Charlotte greeted a customer. Sam quickly added, "I should let you go. Thanks for explaining about the library. It puts my mind at ease."

Charlotte said quietly, "Please keep the bat relocation between us. Once they're safely moved, Diane will file the proper paperwork."

"Of course," Sam promised. "Be careful tonight."

The knot in her shoulders finally loosened. Of course it was about the bats. She'd been imagining conspiracies when the explanation was totally innocent.

Back at home, Sam closed the front door behind her, immediately greeted by Arlo's enthusiastic welcome. His small body wriggled with excitement as he circled her feet, clearly relieved she was finally home.

"I missed you too, buddy," she said, crouching to give him a proper scratch behind the ears. "Sorry I can't take you everywhere with me."

With the seniors relocated to the community center, Sam found herself almost missing Nora's imperious directions and Mrs. Fitzpatrick's Scrabble tournaments. Almost.

She filled Arlo's food bowl while her stomach rumbled a reminder of her own hunger and the fact she hadn't yet eaten breakfast. Opening the refrigerator, she assessed the remains of her perishables. The generator had kept everything cold, but she needed to use items before they spoiled.

After a simple breakfast of scrambled eggs and toast, Sam settled at the kitchen table with her notebook and a cup of tea. There was a lot of comfort for her in organizing her thoughts on paper.

Sam opened her notebook and wrote "Harrison & Kevin: Connections" in her neat handwriting. Below it, she'd drawn lines connecting names: Victor Reid (financial desperation, architectural knowledge), Charlotte Webb (bookstore threatened, family history with hotel), Diane Foster (environmental permits, bat habitat access), Trevor Mills (lost contract, restoration expertise).

She tapped her pen against the paper, then added a new line: "Missing finials. Who had access?" The finial found at the development site made sense, of course. Whoever killed Harrison couldn't bring themselves to destroy something worth thousands of dollars, even if it was a murder weapon. The construction site was a smart choice for temporary storage since the ground was already torn up from construction, and it wasn't far from the hotel. It was a wooded area, and the construction had taken a break lately because of some sort of permit issue with the city. It would be easy to partially bury something quickly and come back for it later.

Sam made a note: "Killer planned to retrieve finial and was interrupted by police investigation?" She paused, looking at the notes. It almost seemed like a puzzle, but not as innocuous. If the killer wasn't caught soon, there could be another death as he got more desperate.

She decided to take a walk over to the clubhouse to clear her head. She also hoped she might be able to get an update on the Alfred and Mandy project. Sam clipped Arlo's leash and they headed out. The little dog seemed eager for the exercise, his tail wagging as they navigated around the remaining storm debris scattered along the sidewalks.

The morning air carried the scent of wet leaves and the distant sound of chainsaws still working to clear fallen trees. Maple Hills was beginning to look like itself again, though blue tarps on roofs and stacks of debris at curbsides served as reminders of what they'd all endured. Sam found herself cataloging the progress as they walked—the Hendersons had removed the tree from their driveway, the Chens had replaced their damaged mailbox, and someone had finally cleared the fallen power line from Cedar Street.

Arlo trotted happily beside her, occasionally stopping to investigate an interesting scent or greet a neighbor working in their yard. Mrs. Patterson waved from her front porch, where she was sweeping away the last of the leaves that had blown against her door.

"Morning, Sam! How's the recovery going?"

"Better every day," Sam called back, meaning it more than she'd expected to when the words left her mouth.

The clubhouse had never been so organized. Sam found Trevor and Nora huddled over paperwork at the main table, Trevor's laptop open showing what appeared to be a spreadsheet. Arlo immediately trotted over to Trevor, who smiled and reached down to scratch behind the dog's ears.

"There you are," Nora announced when Sam walked in. "We're tracking the final contributions for Alfred and Mandy."

"How's it looking?" Sam asked, settling into a chair. Arlo padded over to investigate the corner where someone had thoughtfully placed a water bowl.

Trevor gestured to his screen. "The good news is we're at about seventy-five hundred dollars. Word's been spreading beyond the original meeting."

"Really?" Sam felt a surge of satisfaction. "I was hoping more people would want to contribute once they heard about it."

"Mrs. Chen stopped by this morning with a check," Nora said, consulting her precise notes. "She said she couldn't make the meeting but heard about the scholarship fund from her neighbor. Dave at the hardware store contributed too, plus he's donating materials for smaller repairs."

Trevor nodded. "Alfred asked me to help coordinate the insurance timeline since I've been through this process with other neighbors recently. The adjuster confirmed they can start work as soon as the deductible is paid, but they need it upfront. Alfred, of course, is totally capable of dealing with his insurance, but he asked me to work with the contractors the insurance company is assigning, since I know most of them."

"How much more do we need?" Sam asked.

Nora tapped her pen against her notepad. "About five hundred dollars. I'm confident we'll have it by tomorrow. Three more neighbors said they'd stop by this evening with contributions."

"The timing works perfectly," Trevor added. "I can present the deductible payment to the insurance company Friday morning, and they'll authorize work to begin Monday."

Sam felt the familiar satisfaction of a plan coming together successfully. "When do we surprise them with the news?"

"I suggest this coming Friday," Nora said with characteristic confidence. "Once we have the full amount and can present it as a done deal. Alfred and Mandy won't have time to object or try to refuse."

Trevor's expression grew warm. "You should see how excited Alfred gets when he talks about that scholarship. He mentioned it again yesterday—how they're finally ready to help a local student get technical training."

"That's exactly why this matters," Sam said. "Fifteen years of saving shouldn't disappear because of one storm."

Arlo wandered back over, having completed his investigation of the clubhouse. He settled at Sam's feet with a contented sigh, apparently satisfied that this was a place where good things were happening.

"The tricky part is going to be presenting this to them," Sam said. "Alfred and Mandy are going to want to know exactly how much everyone contributed, and they'll try to find ways to pay people back."

"I've been thinking about that," Nora said. "We should just remind them that we're not giving them money—we're ensuring the scholarship can continue as planned."

Trevor nodded thoughtfully. "That might work. Alfred takes that scholarship seriously."

Sam and Arlo walked home minutes later. When they passed Alfred and Mandy's house, Sam noticed the blue tarp stretched across the damaged section of roof, held down with sandbags. The temporary repair looked professional—probably Alfred's work, making the best of a difficult situation while he waited for permanent solutions. In the backyard, she could see Mandy hanging laundry on a clothesline, making do without her storm-damaged dryer.

Back home from the clubhouse, Sam settled into her favorite chair in the living room with Arlo curling up beside her. She pulled out her phone to check for any messages she might have missed during the walk. Cell service was still spotty, but a text from Aiden had made it through.

Alfred just drove by the gas station—says there's a tanker truck there right now. Lines will be crazy soon. Want to head over now before word spreads?

Sam jumped up, startling Arlo. Her fuel gauge had been nagging at her all week.

She texted back quickly: "On my way! Thanks for the heads up."

Three dots appeared immediately: "See you there."

Sam smiled. Even a mundane gas station meetup felt like something to look forward to these days. And Aiden's steady presence throughout this crisis had been comforting. More than comforting, if she was honest with herself. But that was a list for another day.

Chapter Twenty-Four

Sam grabbed her keys and headed for the car, Arlo looking up hopefully from his favorite sunny spot on the kitchen floor.

"Sorry, buddy. Just a boring gas run," she said, giving him a pat. "I'll be back soon."

The streets were busier now than they had been in the early morning, with neighbors out working in their yards and small convoys of repair trucks navigating around remaining debris. Sam could see the progress Maple Hills was making—more blue tarps had been replaced with actual roof repairs, and most of the major tree limbs had been cleared from the main roads.

When Sam arrived at the gas station, she was relieved to see only three cars ahead of her in line. The tanker truck was still there, its driver methodically checking connections while the station attendant prepared to start pumping.

She pulled in and was pleased to spot Aiden walking toward her car from the convenience store, coffee cup in hand.

"Perfect timing," he said, approaching her driver's side window. "I got a couple of coffees for us to drink while we wait. Want one?"

"That would be great," Sam replied, rolling down her window. "How long have you been here?"

"About ten minutes. Alfred wasn't kidding—word's already spreading. There are at least six more cars pulling in behind you."

Sam glanced in her rearview mirror to see the line growing rapidly. "Good call on rushing over."

Aiden stood outside her car while Sam waited for her turn at the pump, steam rising from their coffee cups in the cool air.

"How's your day been?" Aiden asked, leaning against Sam's car.

"Really well, actually," Sam replied. "I ran by to see Charlotte this morning. That meeting Olivia overheard between Diane and Charlotte was about relocating the bats from the hotel to the old library. Victor is apparently helping them out with that."

"Oh, that's good. So no skullduggery, just environmental work."

Sam said, "That's right. Which is great, because I hated thinking Charlotte was somehow involved in all this. Then I checked in at the clubhouse. Nora's just five hundred dollars shy of the deductible amount." Sam smiled. "I think we can actually pull this off without Alfred and Mandy having to touch their savings."

"That's amazing. They've done so much for this community over the years."

The car ahead of Sam finished pumping and pulled away. "Looks like I'm up," she said, moving her car forward to the pump.

"I should head out anyway," Aiden said, checking his watch. "I promised to help clear storm debris from the elementary school playground."

Sam smiled as she got out to pump her gas. "Thanks for the coffee and the company."

"Anytime," he replied, climbing into his truck. "See you later."

After Aiden left and Sam finished filling her tank, she decided to drive past the construction site where they had found the finial yesterday. She was curious whether the police had discovered anything else, and it was on her way home.

The construction site was quiet, the yellow police tape still visible around the area where they had found the finial and Kevin's camera. Sam slowed as she approached, noticing with surprise a dark blue pickup truck parked half-hidden behind a stand of trees near the site.

She pulled over, keeping a cautious distance. The truck looked similar to the one Lucy had described seeing speed away yesterday morning. It definitely was not a police vehicle.

Sam debated what to do. She tried calling Chief Hawkins, but her phone showed "No Service" at the edge of her screen. The cell towers were still unreliable in this part of town. She looked in her purse for her walkie-talkie before realizing she'd left the house in too much of a rush for the gasoline and had left it behind.

As she weighed her options, she noticed movement near where the finial had been found. Someone was crouched in the brush, digging frantically in the soil. The figure was slender, wearing a dark hoodie pulled up despite the growing warmth of the morning.

Sam slid down in her seat slightly, observing from a distance. Something about the person's movements seemed familiar. When they stood and pushed back their hood to wipe their forehead, Sam caught a glimpse of their face and felt a jolt of surprise.

Angie Mills.

What was Trevor's daughter digging around a crime scene?

Sam took a few photos with her phone, thinking they might be useful for the police. She was about to start her car and leave to find help when Angie turned in her direction. Their eyes met across the distance, and Angie froze.

For a moment, neither moved. Then Angie quickly grabbed a tire iron from the truck bed and started walking purposefully toward Sam's car.

Chapter Twenty-Five

Her heart hammered against her ribs. The access road behind her was churned into a muddy mess from yesterday's rain and construction vehicles. She'd made it in by driving carefully, but backing out fast would be treacherous. One wrong move and she'd be stuck in the mud, completely helpless.

Angie's heavy pickup had better traction. If she tried to flee and got stuck, she'd be a sitting duck.

Think, Sam. Think.

The tire iron glinted in Angie's hand. Sweet, helpful Angie who'd walked Arlo and organized supplies at the clubhouse. How had she missed it? Her mouth went dry. She was alone with a killer, and no one knew where she was.

The car door handle felt cold under her palm. Getting out seemed insane, but being trapped in her car felt worse. At least outside she could move, could run if she had to. And maybe, if she was lucky, she could make it to solid ground before Angie reached her. At the very least, she could scope out the area.

Taking a deep breath, Sam stepped out of her car, keeping the door open between them as a barrier. She maintained her composure, though her heart hammered in her chest.

"Hi, Angie," she called, trying to sound casual. "What brings you out here?"

Angie stopped about fifteen feet away, the tire iron gripped tightly in her hand. The girl Sam knew had vanished, replaced by someone whose eyes darted nervously between Sam and the dig site.

"I could ask you the same thing," Angie replied, her voice tight.

"I'm just heading back from filling up the car," Sam said truthfully. "I noticed your truck and was curious. This is still a crime scene."

Angie's knuckles whitened around the tire iron. "You need to leave, Sam. Now."

The pieces clicked into place in Sam's mind—Angie's photography work documenting buildings around town, her access to her father's construction knowledge, her desperate need for college money after losing her scholarship. Her boyfriend with a truck.

"You were looking for something else buried here," Sam said quietly. "Something besides the finial they found yesterday."

Angie's expression confirmed Sam's suspicion before she could hide it. "You don't know what you're talking about."

"I think I do," Sam replied, carefully reaching for her keys in her pocket. "You know a lot about architecture from working with your father. Your senior project even involves architecture. But you weren't just taking pictures, were you?"

"Stop talking," Angie said, taking a step closer.

"Kevin had photos on his camera," Sam continued, keeping her voice steady. "Before and after shots of the hotel. He knew someone was stealing them and how valuable they were. Maybe he also realized he had a picture of you somewhere on the premises."

Angie swung the tire iron in a small arc by her side. "It wasn't supposed to happen like this," she said, her voice cracking.

"Like what?" Sam asked.

"I just needed money for college. After my scholarship fell through, Dad couldn't help much with tuition." Angie's eyes darted toward the dig site, then back to Sam.

"So you started removing architectural elements from the hotel," Sam said, watching as Angie's knuckles whitened around the tire iron. She quickly glanced around to see if there was a good spot to run out. But she'd have to run toward the hotel, where most of the guests were now gone. And Angie was younger and probably faster.

"Five thousand dollars for a finial doesn't sound like much for college," Angie said. "But when you're going to State and you've got four or five pieces to sell? That's a semester of tuition and books right there." There was a hint of pride in her voice. "I had buyers lined up through online forums. There are plenty of collectors who pay premium prices for original Victorian finials with the right patina."

"Until Harrison caught you," Sam said. She looked behind Angie, on the other end of the construction site. She didn't see any nearby businesses in that direction to run to. Plus, there was a chain-link fence.

Angie's face hardened. "He showed up that night during the storm when I was removing the east corner finial." She looked away. "He said he was going to call the police and have me arrested for theft and destruction of property." Her laugh was bitter. "Like he hadn't been destroying the town's history himself with his bulldozers and cheap materials."

Sam noticed the chain-link fence had taken a hit during the storm. Part of it was missing. Enough, maybe, for her to drive through. She took a small step toward her car door. "You must have been furious."

"Dad did the restoration work on that hotel five years ago," Angie said. "He taught me everything about that decorative ironwork. Which ones were original, which ones were valuable. When he lost the new renovation bid to Harrison's out-of-state company, he was really upset."

"That must have been hard to watch," Sam said, poised to spring for the car when she had a chance.

"Dad would still get called in occasionally when the new contractors needed his expertise on the historical features," Angie continued. "It was humiliating for him."

"And that's how you got access," Sam concluded.

Angie nodded. "It was easy. I'd drive Dad to the site when he got consulting calls, take my camera, and tell everyone I was documenting it for my senior project. Nobody questions a kid with a camera whose father is right there working." She twisted the tire iron in her hands. "Then I'd come back later, use the access codes I'd memorized, climb the scaffolding they'd already set up, and take what I needed."

"And Harrison caught you in the act," Sam said.

"It was an accident," Angie insisted, more to herself than to Sam. "He grabbed me, and I just reacted. The finial was right there in my hands. He tried to take it from me."

"Which is how his clothing ended up with those zinc markings on it," said Sam.

"Whatever. I hit him with it, then left with the finial."

"What about Kevin?" asked Sam.

"Kevin called me a few days ago," Angie said, her voice tight. "He said he had photos of someone on the hotel roof and wanted to give me a chance to explain before he went to the police. He asked me to meet him there." Her laugh was bitter. "I thought maybe I could convince him to keep quiet, that I'd pay him back or something. But when I got there, he was up on the scaffolding taking more pictures. He said he was calling someone for backup—that he didn't want to handle this alone." She swallowed hard. "I knew I only had minutes before help arrived. I climbed up to try to grab his camera, and we struggled. I just . . . pushed him. I didn't mean for him to fall."

Sam saw her opportunity as Angie was lost in the memory. She quickly slipped into her car and locked the doors, jamming the key into the ignition. Before she could start the engine, Angie rushed forward, swinging the tire iron at the driver's side window. The safety glass spiderwebbed but held.

Sam started the car as Angie raised the tire iron for another blow. She couldn't risk backing out through the muddy access road. Instead, she threw the car into drive and lurched forward, straight at Angie.

Angie dove aside, slipping in the mud and falling hard. Sam gunned the engine, bumping over the uneven construction ground toward a gap in the chain-link fence she had noticed. Behind her, she saw Angie scrambling to her feet.

The gap in the fence was narrower than it had appeared. Sam squeezed her car through, wincing at the scraping sound along the sides. The offroad drive was bumpy, but she made it onto the connecting road and solid pavement at last.

In her rearview mirror, she saw Angie racing back to her truck, mud-streaked and furious. The blue pickup roared to life, but Angie had to navigate carefully around the muddy construction site to reach the exit. She apparently opted not to try her luck with the fence.

Sam accelerated on the paved road, putting precious distance between herself and Angie's pursuing truck. The road curved sharply ahead, following the natural contour of the hillside. Sam took the turn carefully, while Angie's heavier truck took it too fast, sliding partially off the shoulder. It gave Sam even more lead time.

She checked her phone again, but there was still no service. She headed straight to the police station.

The modest brick building that housed the Sunset Ridge Police Department came into view as Sam navigated the final turn. She pulled into the parking lot fast, laying on her horn as she spotted Officer Martinez walking toward her patrol car.

"Officer Martinez!" Sam shouted, jumping out of her car. "That truck is chasing me. Angie Mills tried to kill me."

Martinez immediately dropped into action mode, hand moving to her weapon as she spotted Angie's pickup roaring into the parking lot behind Sam.

Angie saw the patrol car and tried to veer away, but her truck skidded on the wet pavement and slammed into a concrete planter at the lot's edge. Steam rose from the crumpled hood.

Martinez was moving before the truck stopped, weapon drawn. "Hands where I can see them! Out of the vehicle, now!"

Sam watched from behind Martinez's cruiser as a dazed Angie stumbled out of the smoking truck, hands raised.

"Angie Mills," Martinez said as she approached with handcuffs. "You're under arrest."

That's when Sam spotted Trevor Mills pulling into the parking lot across the street, his work truck loaded with tools as he headed for the paint shop. His face went white as he stepped out and took in the scene—his daughter in handcuffs, the crashed truck, and the police weapon.

"Angie?" His voice cracked as he got out of his work truck. "What's happening?"

Chief Hawkins emerged from the station, drawn by the commotion. After a quick assessment of the scene, he approached Trevor.

"Mr. Mills, I'm sorry you had to see this," the chief said quietly. "We need to talk."

"Dad, I'm sorry," Angie said as Martinez led her toward the station entrance. "I'm so sorry."

Trevor stood frozen, watching his daughter being escorted inside, his expression cycling through confusion, disbelief, and dawning horror.

Chapter Twenty-Six

Twenty minutes later, Chief Hawkins took her statement. Sam sat in the police station, hands still shaking slightly as she recounted everything that had happened.

"She admitted to killing both of them. Harrison caught her removing the finial during the storm, and she hit him with it. Then Kevin recognized her from his photo and started asking questions," said Sam.

"We found more finials in a storage unit rented under a fake name," Chief Hawkins told her. "The paperwork matches samples of Angie's handwriting."

Sam shook her head. "I don't understand why she hid the finial at the construction site instead of at the storage units."

"I asked Angie the same thing. She said it was because she panicked after killing Harrison. The site was close and the storage building was across town. She planned on coming back later after things had calmed down."

"It's just hard for me to believe she was under our noses all the time," Sam said, remembering Angie walking Arlo, helping at the clubhouse, cheerfully taking pictures of storm damage around town.

"Best disguise there is," the chief replied. "People see what they expect to see. Nobody expects the helpful teenager with the camera." He paused. "You displayed some quick thinking today. Not many people would've kept their wits about them in your situation. I'd like you to text someone to pick you up, though. I know the cell service isn't stable, but you might be able to get through."

Sam nodded, taking a stab at texting with her trembling hands. She wasn't at all sure she'd reach Aiden, but he immediately said he was on his way.

"What will happen to Angie?" Sam asked, her voice quiet.

"She's facing some serious charges," the chief replied. "Two counts of homicide is just the beginning. We'll be searching that storage unit thoroughly and contacting her online buyers."

Sam nodded, her thoughts drifting back to Trevor. The contractor had stood motionless, watching his daughter being taken away. His shoulders were slumped, his face etched with confusion and grief.

"Trevor had no idea," Sam said. "You can see it in his face."

"We'll question him thoroughly," Chief Hawkins assured her. "But initial evidence suggests she acted alone. The irony is that Trevor taught her everything she needed to know without realizing how she would use that knowledge."

"Was Angie's boyfriend involved? I know she borrowed his truck to collect the finials."

"We questioned him right off the bat, worried he might make a run for it if he was an accomplice. But Angie told him she needed the truck to help out her dad and get photos for the school paper on the storm damage. Her car battery is still dead and since the auto shops closed without power, Trevor hasn't had a chance to get another. He seems to have no idea what she was really doing."

A knock on the interview room door interrupted them. Officer Martinez peered in. "Chief? Aiden Wood is here for Ms. Prescott."

"That was fast," Chief Hawkins said, rising from his chair. "We're done here for now, anyway. I'll need you to come back tomorrow to sign your formal statement, but you're free to go."

Sam stood on unsteady legs, the adrenaline finally wearing off. "Thank you, Chief."

In the station's lobby, Aiden was waiting with barely contained worry etched across his face. The moment he saw her, relief flooded his features.

"Sam," he said, crossing to her immediately. "Are you okay?"

"I will be," she told him as his hand found hers, warm and steadying. The simple contact helped ground her after the chaos of the afternoon.

Aiden's eyes searched her face with concern. "When I got your text, I was scared something had happened to you."

"Can you drive me home?" Sam asked. "My car's evidence now, apparently. And Arlo's probably wondering where I am. I was just supposed to be getting gas."

"Of course," Aiden said immediately. "Come on, let's get you home."

The drive back to her house was quiet with Aiden occasionally glancing over to check on her. As they pulled into her driveway, Sam finally spoke.

"I keep thinking about how desperate Angie must have been. College money, her father struggling after losing that contract to Harrison." Sam shook her head. "She had all the knowledge from working with Trevor, access to the hotel through his consulting work, and buyers lined up online. It probably seemed like the perfect solution."

"Until Harrison caught her in the act," Aiden said quietly.

"And then Kevin started asking questions about his photo." Sam's voice was heavy. "Two people died because an eighteen-year-old was trying to pay for college."

As they reached her front door, Arlo's excited barking greeted them from inside. The familiar sound brought a smile to Sam's face despite the morning's events.

"I can stay for a while if you want company," Aiden offered, his voice gentle. "Or I can go if you need space."

Sam considered for a moment. Normally, she would have chosen solitude to process everything that had happened. But today, the thought of being alone held no appeal.

"I could use some company," she admitted. "And I think Arlo would appreciate a walk after being cooped up all morning."

Aiden smiled, relieved. "I can definitely help with that."

As she unlocked the door, Sam felt the weight of the past few days begin to lift slightly. The storm had passed. The murders were solved. And while Sunset Ridge had a long road to recovery ahead, Sam found herself looking forward to whatever came next—especially if it involved the man standing beside her.

Arlo bounded out to greet them, his whole body wiggling with joy. Sam knelt to ruffle his ears, drawing comfort from his uncomplicated happiness.

Days later, the community was gradually finding its rhythm again. Sam stood at the edge of Franklin's makeshift agility course, where the agility club had gathered for their first post-storm practice. Lucy's whippet Ziggy raced through the tunnel of tarps while Dave adjusted the branch hurdles.

"This is actually pretty impressive," Lucy said, her enthusiastic voice carrying across the field as she waved toward Franklin, who was beaming with pride. "The kid's got a talent for course design."

"He came up with this after seeing the damage to our regular field," Sam said. "He turned storm debris into something positive."

Across the field, Arlo greeted each club member in turn, his tail wagging as he moved from person to person. Sam spotted Victor Reid watching from the edge of the gathering. Aiden had invited him as part of his ongoing effort to help the historian reconnect with the community.

"Arlo's making his rounds," Aiden commented, joining Sam with two paper cups of coffee. "He knows exactly who needs a friendly face today."

Sam accepted the coffee gratefully. "He was especially gentle with Trevor when we ran into him downtown."

The memory of Trevor's haunted expression still tugged at her heart. The contractor had been devastated by recent events, but the community had rallied around him in ways Sam hadn't expected. Meals appeared on his doorstep and neighbors offered work.

"The field should be ready in a few weeks," Ginny said, watching Franklin demonstrate the course for the younger club members. "I told Franklin I'd run through ideas for the course with him. The kid's got a knack for this."

Chapter Twenty-Seven

On Friday, Sam made sure she and Arlo were at Alfred and Mandy's house at the appointed time. A large group of neighbors and others from the town had gathered in the yard. Sam rang the doorbell, and then Alfred and Mandy stood on their front porch, staring at the envelope in Alfred's weathered hands. The blue tarp still covered the damaged section of their roof, and water stains were visible on the porch ceiling where rain had gotten through. Slowly, Alfred opened the envelope.

"I don't understand," Mandy said quietly, her voice unsteady. "Eight thousand dollars?"

Sam stood with the gathered neighbors. "Consider it a community investment in your scholarship fund," she said with a smile.

Trevor stepped forward with a folder. He looked older than he had and fine lines creased his face. "I spoke with your insurance company this morning. They'll start the roof work Monday, and the deductible payment clears the way for everything to be covered."

"The deductible?" Alfred's voice was rough. "But we were going to use the scholarship money—"

"Now you don't have to," Sam said gently. "Your scholarship can happen exactly as you planned."

Nora adjusted her glasses with characteristic authority. "We simply couldn't allow fifteen years of your generosity to be derailed by one storm," she said with a huff.

Alfred held the check with shaking hands. Mandy peered over his shoulder, then pressed her hand to her mouth.

"The scholarship is supposed to be awarded next month," Mandy managed. "We'd already started reviewing applications."

"And now you still can," Sam said. "Without having to choose between your home and your dream of helping someone else."

Alfred cleared his throat several times, his usual gruff composure completely gone. "I don't know what to say."

"You could tell us about the scholarship," Sam suggested. "About why it matters to you."

Alfred looked at Mandy, who nodded encouragingly. "My father was a janitor," he began, his voice growing stronger. "Smartest man I ever knew, but never had the chance for education. When our nephew Jimmy wanted electrical training but couldn't afford it, that hit me hard." He swallowed. "Mandy and I decided no one should be stopped by money if they had the will to learn."

"Fifteen years of saving," Mandy whispered, looking at the check again. "We can actually do this."

"You were always going to do this," Sam said. "We just made sure the storm didn't get in the way."

Alfred approached her as neighbors began to drift toward their cars. "Sam," he said simply, extending his hand.

She took it, expecting a handshake, but found herself pulled into a fierce hug instead.

"Thank you," Alfred said gruffly.

A few minutes later, she and Arlo walked back home. Arlo trotted happily beside her, occasionally stopping to investigate an interesting scent or greet another dog.

As they rounded the corner and were in front of Olivia's house, Sam spotted Olivia walking up her driveway, carrying a box of decorations for the upcoming fall festival. In the wake of the hurricane, the town council had decided that Sunset Ridge needed something to celebrate, and the annual tradition had taken on new significance.

"Need a hand with that?" Sam called.

Olivia turned, her face lighting up. "Hey there. Sure, that would be great."

They worked together to carry the decorations inside, falling into the easy rhythm of friendship that had deepened through shared crisis. In the kitchen, Sam noticed a familiar list on Olivia's refrigerator—one of Sam's organizational systems adapted to Olivia's handwriting.

"You're still using my checklists," Sam observed with a smile.

"They work," Olivia said simply. "I've even started making my own for the food bank." She hesitated. "Trevor looked exhausted at Alfred and Mandy's. I really feel for him."

"Trevor's been trying to get into a routine, I think. He's visiting Angie during visiting hours, but really needed work to help keep him centered. He's accepted that renovation contract for the old library."

"People need purpose after loss," Olivia said softly, her own experience with grief evident in her voice. "It helps to have something to rebuild."

As Sam walked home later, she reflected on how much had changed since the storm first hit. Tragedy had revealed both the worst and best in their community. The same streets that had been flooded and broken were now clearing, with neighbors working side by side to restore what had been damaged.

Her phone buzzed with a text from Aiden: "Still on for dinner? Made reservations at Highland Grill. First night they're reopened."

Sam smiled, typing back: "Wouldn't miss it. Arlo and I just finished our walk."

Three dots appeared, then: "Looking forward to seeing you both."

When she reached her home, Sam paused on the veranda, taking in the view of Maple Hills. The houses below showed signs of repair—new roofs, fresh paint, rebuilt porches. Between the crisis response and the investigation, she hadn't taken much time to appreciate how far they'd all come.

Inside, she added one final item to her recovery checklist: "Remember to celebrate progress." Then she drew a firm line through it, already complete.

Arlo padded into the room, his leash in his mouth, always ready for the next adventure. Sam laughed, scratching his ears. "Not quite yet, buddy. We've got time."

And for the first time since the hurricane hit, that felt absolutely true.

About the Author

Bestselling cozy mystery author Elizabeth Spann Craig is a library-loving, avid mystery reader. A pet-owning Southerner, her four series are full of cats, corgis, and cheese grits. The mother of two, she lives with her husband, a fun-loving corgi, and a couple of cute cats.

Sign up for Elizabeth's free newsletter to stay updated on releases:

https://bit.ly/2xZUXqO

This and That

I love hearing from my readers. You can find me on Facebook as Elizabeth Spann Craig Author, on Twitter as elizabethscraig, on my website at elizabethspanncraig.com, and by email at elizabethspanncraig@gmail.com.

Thanks so much for reading my book...I appreciate it. If you enjoyed the story, would you please leave a short review on the site where you purchased it? Just a few words would be great. Not only do I feel encouraged reading them, but they also help other readers discover my books. Thank you!

Did you know my books are available in print and ebook formats? Most of the Myrtle Clover series is available in audio and some of the Southern Quilting mysteries are. Find the audiobooks here: https://elizabethspanncraig.com/audio/

Please follow me on BookBub for my reading recommendations and release notifications.

I'd also like to thank some folks who helped me put this book together. Thanks to my cover designer, Karri Klawiter, for her awesome covers. Thanks to my editor, Judy Beatty for her help. Thanks to beta readers Amanda Arrieta, Rebecca Wahr, Cassie Kelley, and Dan Harris for all of their helpful suggestions and careful reading. Thanks to my ARC readers for helping to spread the word. Thanks, as always, to my family and readers.

Other Works by Elizabeth

Myrtle Clover Series in Order (be sure to look for the Myrtle series in audio, ebook, and print):

Pretty is as Pretty Dies
Progressive Dinner Deadly
A Dyeing Shame
A Body in the Backyard
Death at a Drop-In
A Body at Book Club
Death Pays a Visit
A Body at Bunco
Murder on Opening Night
Cruising for Murder
Cooking is Murder
A Body in the Trunk
Cleaning is Murder
Edit to Death
Hushed Up
A Body in the Attic
Murder on the Ballot
Death of a Suitor

A Dash of Murder
Death at a Diner
A Myrtle Clover Christmas
Murder at a Yard Sale
Doom and Bloom
A Toast to Murder
Mystery Loves Company (2025)

THE VILLAGE LIBRARY Mysteries in Order (and in audio):
Checked Out
Overdue
Borrowed Time
Hush-Hush
Where There's a Will
Frictional Characters
Spine Tingling
A Novel Idea
End of Story
Booked Up
Out of Circulation
Shelf Life (2025)

The Sunset Ridge Mysteries in Order
The Type-A Guide to Solving Murder
The Type-A Guide to Dinner Parties (2025)

Southern Quilting Mysteries in Order:
Quilt or Innocence

Knot What it Seams
Quilt Trip
Shear Trouble
Tying the Knot
Patch of Trouble
Fall to Pieces
Rest in Pieces
On Pins and Needles
Fit to be Tied
Embroidering the Truth
Knot a Clue
Quilt-Ridden
Needled to Death
A Notion to Murder
Crosspatch
Behind the Seams
Quilt Complex
A Southern Quilting Cozy Christmas

MEMPHIS BARBEQUE MYSTERIES in Order (Written as Riley Adams):
Delicious and Suspicious
Finger Lickin' Dead
Hickory Smoked Homicide
Rubbed Out

And a standalone "cozy zombie" novel: Race to Refuge, written as Liz Craig